D0648830

THE SILVER BUGLE

A SOUND *of* TREASON

R. NORTON HALL, M.D.

authorHOUSE®

AuthorHouse™
1663 Liberty Drive
Bloomington, IN 47403
www.authorhouse.com
Phone: 833-262-8899

Published by AuthorHouse 11/28/2020

ISBN: 978-1-7283-7143-6 (sc)
ISBN: 978-1-7283-7243-3 (e)

Library of Congress Control Number: 2020916591

Print information available on the last page.

DEDICATION

To My son Bruce, a disabled "Devil Dog,"
and all those who serve, now, will and have served
in the armed forces and as first responders.

ACKNOWLEDGMENTS

My gratitude to Elizabeth Bancroft, Managing Editor of The Intelligencer, Journal of U.S. Intelligence Studies, advisor superiore and editor extraordinaire, she was the matriarch of the manuscript. Allen C. Guelzo, Henry R. Luce Professor of Civil War Era and Director of Civil War Era Studies at Gettysburg College, now distinguished Professor at the James Madison Institute of Princeton University, was kind enough to allow me to tap into his encyclopedic cerebrum through the years of keeping poetic license at a minimum in writing this tale. David Connolly is the computer wizard who dragged this electronic dinosaur through the swamp of electronic misery and monsters. And to all the good people at AuthorHouse, Logan Burton, Melanie Lear, Kristine Mayo and Leigh Allen, whose patience has been tried but not found wanting. To all these people and scores of others who helped along this long journey, I want you to know that you labored for one not so foolish to be ungrateful.

THE WHITE HOUSE OF THE CONFEDERACY. AUGUST 1861

"I knew him well, he worked for me in the War Department---a strange sort, the kind you just couldn't feel free and comfortable around. But he was very keen of mind and intellect, placed second in his class at West Point, the youngest cadet.....got around the age requirement through family connections.... of the Philadelphia elite, father a famous surgeon." Jefferson Davis, President of the Confederate States of America, dropped the New York Herald newspaper on his desk. That newspaper, like most of the major northern papers, had no trouble reaching Richmond in a day or so after publication, and so it remained mysteriously during the course of the war.

Judah Benjamin had brought the paper announcing Lincoln's appointment of Major General George Brinton McClellan to be the commanding general of the Union army and extolling his virtues for having won some minor victories in western Virginia. Minor as they were, they were still victories, something sorely missing in the conduct of the war for the Union forces. Benjamin listened with great interest.

"I am concerned Excellency." Benjamin spoke, " He is indeed a threat to us but to what degree? What do you know of him, his strengths and weaknesses, his ambitions and desires, his temperament and demeanor? And what are his interests off the battlefield, in art, literature, history, philosophy? I am, Excellency, convinced that your gifts of mental acuity and clarity of vision have pictured a future military melodrama in which General

George McClellan will play a major role as our foe for sometime to come."

"So sir, I will continue my deposition." He paused, thought for a moment and then resumed, "No, 'exposition' is what I am constructing... to build a body of knowledge that will insure our ability to force him to leave the future fields of battle in ignominious defeat. Alas, the battlefield. What do we know of his battlefield leadership? Is he competent in battle, a strategist or a tactician, a warring general or a planning general? How is he regarded by his troops and his other generals and officers? Is he capable of following the orders of his superiors including the commander in chief? Is he an aggressive warrior or a reticent decision maker....orders from the safety of the rear? And here is the most significant truth to know...his politics, yes, dear Sir, what about his politics?" Benjamin was now standing in front of the president's desk, hands akimbo with his potbelly abutting the edge of the desk, when a slight blush began to emerge from beneath the edge of his beard and a pinch of perspiration appeared on his brow, neither occurrence effecting a change in the perpetuity of his characteristic smirk.

Jefferson Davis leaned forward, rubbed his chronic bothersome left eye and replied, "Benjamin, my dear fellow, you always sound as if you're in court giving a summation for the defense in a murder trial."

"Hurrah,Hurrah," shouted Judah Benjamin," your Excellency offers an accurate and appropriate analogy. This is a murder case. This general has already invaded our land and murdered our people."

"Come, my friend," Davis counselled, "doomsday is not tomorrow or next week. We will see in good time what our fresh, new, young and bright general brings to us on the field. But I feel obligated to share with you some of my thoughts about him. Now that he is the enemy and no longer of my staff, I am free of the ordinance of respecting and protecting the dignity and privacy of one's subordinates. As I said, he worked under me at War and he was good at what he did, or that's how his reports read. But I always had a sense of unease about him. I don't know why but it was there and I consider myself excelled in early and accurate appraisal of a man's character. He ran his pennant up the flagpole higher than any of his peers, subordinates or superiors whenever there was an opportunity for his advancement." He chuckled, a rare occurrence for the President, "I used him for my purposes. He was cunning but guarded his flanks and had a bevy of reasons---'no excuses sir but reasons,' for a substandard performance or failure of mission. He was a master of detail but never had enough time to get enough facts. His reports were voluminous and self aggrandizing. Decisions were the tardy products of elaborate preparations. That's why I sent him to Crimea as an observer---no initiative required, just report on what you see and hear. And he is fluent in French." He paused, paced about silently and appeared to be in another place at another time.

"Carry on sir, please." Benjamin sank back into his chair, eyes fixed on his President, anxious for any inside information substantiated or not, salacious or not, tidbits, some of half truths, the more the better because Judah Benjamin loved gossip and rumors; it was his main source of useful intelligence in making his way through the biased halls of government in Baton Rouge, Washington, Montgomery and now Richmond.

"At West Point," Davis continued, "he was known as a martinet, rigid in his military bearing and demeanor especially with the lower classmen, took obvious pleasure and went to means so that his intimates knew that his Cadet Manual of Regulations was second only to the Episcopal Book of Common Prayer....he lived by the regs and told you so. He associated mostly with the rich southern plantation owners' sons who seemed to tolerate his idiosyncrasies more comfortably than his northern brethren. By the way, as I said before Benjamin, he was fluent in French, you and he would get on well together."

Benjamin smiled. "Sir, please continue."

"His plebe roommate, A.P. Hill, was almost a complete opposite, but they became close friends and Hill was like the big protective brother. Hill was a frequent patron of Benny Haven's off-limits tavern in the tiny town of Highland Falls just outside the main gate of West Point. The more adventuresome cadets would sneak there after "lights out" to frolic with the local femme fatales. He loved the ladies and had many in his stables, all happy and willing fillies. McClellan never set foot in Benny Haven's and was reticent in dealing with the opposite sex. Hill left for a year because of illness, rumored but unconfirmed, to be complications of gonorrhea, and returned in the class behind McClellan but their friendship was maintained."

Benjamin stirred in his chair, cocking his head so as to not lose a syllable of Jefferson's words; this was grist for Benjamin's mill.

"In the meantime Hill met and fell in love with the belle of the academy cotillions, the daughter of a regular army staff officer at the academy. Neither parent liked Hill and openly denigrated him and endeavored to get her involved with McClellan who was not unwilling but not active or reactive in the process. Matters got serious for the couple and worse for the girl's family when the engagement to be married was announced. In the meantime McClellan and Hill were graduated and serving their tours at their respective duty stations. The Major, Marcy was his name, exerted as much pressure as he could to break up the engagement while his wife was courting McClellan by post.'

"Your Excellency, this is preposterous," Benjamin interrupted. "You mean to say that Mrs. Marcy was having a tryst by post with young McClellan?...Truly absurd, unbelievable and obscene."

"Oh no no Judah," calling Benjamin by his first name for the first time in a long time, "she wasn't courting George, she was the interlocutor. He was courting the daughter indirectly through his letters to her mother who was a willing participant in this strange triangle of love and intrigue.....a postmistress of sorts, a Cupidess if you will." and he chuckled.

Benjamin, wiped his brow, enthralled and anxiously awaiting the next word.

Davis continued, "Hill was unaware of the intensity of the Marcy family's involvement with McClellan. Eventually, the father prevailed, the engagement was broken, and Hill was crushed. George then initiated real courting instead of the proxy variety through the mother. He proposed marriage a couple of times and was rejected. He persisted, she relented, the family was happy, the date was set and the ceremony took place. But the story doesn't end there. Mind you Judah, just my stilted view from a distance, but I think A.P. and the Marcy girl are still in love."

Judah Benjamin was apoplectic.

Davis was excited with an element of joy, like no other time witnessed by Judah Benjamin. He stopped pacing and wiped his oozing eye, "As you know, Hill also worked for me and was a self-motivated engine of activity. Before he was fully briefed on a mission, he was on his way to accomplish it and accomplish it he did. He was admired, respected, and well liked by all."

Jefferson Davis, by listening to his own words about the man he would face leading the forces of the foe, a man he thought he knew well, had generated a heretofore unappreciated presence of a gift...a gift that few battlefield commanders were presented. He knew his enemy before a battle was fought. He smiled and thought to himself, "I won't look this gift horse in the mouth." Suddenly his mood was disturbed by Benjamin's voice.

"This is profoundly interesting and fascinating your Excellency," Benjamin stage-whispered as he shifted forward in his chair, gaze fixed on his narrator's countenance. "Tell me more sir, my brain is a wanting beast."

"What is so beguiling about this Judah?" Davis asked as if what he had just related was, at best, an interesting distraction from what really matters at the moment, meeting the challenges of running a new government.

"Mr. President sir, please forgive me." Benjamin's dark beady eyes were blazing under fully arched eyebrows, "For you see, sir, in the dark nether of my mind, a spark has been ignited. What you've related about the general, his wife and Hill has advanced that spark to light a lamp that illuminates an unfolding drama that could be our salvation in the coming firestorm of mortal conflict. My thoughts are running in my head like a herd of wild mustangs and I beg to take your leave. I am quite convinced, as you stated, that the story didn't end there and it hasn't ended yet....and in my opinion kind sir, it will go on for sometime hopefully enriched by the thoughtful additions of some well placed influences of the Confederacy. I will join you at our appointed luncheon. Good day sir." And he left.

Jefferson Davis walked over to the window of his office in his new official residence, the White House of the Confederacy. He glanced down on the new government worker bees buzzing about the corner of Clay and 12th streets in Richmond's Court End section. There was much to do in meeting the increasing demands of the new government at war with an adversary that was superior in numbers, supplies, and treasure. And this while trying to complete a smooth transition of moving a functional seat of government from its capital in Montgomery, Alabama to Richmond, Virginia. "Less interference up here than down there and I enjoy the convenience of having office and home in the same place," he thought aloud.

A Plot Inseminated

Separated from each other physically but not so in thought, both Davis and Benjamin were ruminating about the day's earlier conversation about General McClellan. There was so much more Davis could have told Benjamin about young George...his driving ambition, his need to be the great one, his poorly disguised sense of superiority, his obvious display of spirituality and that God was his guide and always on his side. He wasn't always right but, in all humility, he couldn't remember whenever he was wrong. His brass always had to display the brightest sheen.

And strangely, despite how those amorous things worked out, both Hill, a Virginia farm boy, a hunter and horseman, and McClellan, a scion of a socialite Philadelphia surgeon, were still close friends and corresponded frequently.

Benjamin couldn't take his mind off of the morning's conversation and the President's detailed account of McClellan...full of facts and feelings that weren't fully stated but the essence was there... and picked up by the wily Judah Benjamin, master of the Senate cloakroom secrets and manipulator of men, denizen of the dissemblers. Our young Napoleon was strong in self importance but not so strong in trust. He was comfortable in the bright lights of power and wealth but also in the penumbra of the economy of truth. As far as Judah Benjamin was concerned, General George Brinton McClellan was a study to be pursued.

McClellan was familiar with all, friendly with most, and intimate with a few of the southern cadets who resigned from the U.S. Army and volunteered to the Confederacy at the initiation of hostilities in 1861. Cadet bonds were strong and some ties were eternal as sworn to by some. Thus, thought Judah Benjamin that General McClellan should be considered to be approached as a friend in perpetuity to his cadet classmates and colleagues of Southern sympathy and, better yet, as a surreptitious apostle in rendering information to preserve and protect the lives, culture and peace of his beloved brethren of the Point. This to save them from the annihilating and murderous invasions of the abominable abolitionists and anti-states righters from New England and Washington. Aside from the absolute Christian and moral grounds for his contributions to the offering plate, God's grace would be forthcoming also providing access to personal rewards, military, historic, political and economic.

At the appointed luncheon both men appeared unduly tense and conversation appeared stilted. Smiles were forced and brief. Thank God Varina Davis, the President's articulate, beautiful and cultured wife was in attendance. Above all, a God send for that occasion; she was a brilliant conversationalist. Most of the talk centered around the recent move from Montgomery, Alabama and the rigors of resettling her husband, the children, servants, government staff, soldiers and, finally, herself. "It was truly," she said, "a labor of love for all involved but for husband and children it was a labor of love enduring and everlasting." The President smiled warmly and nodded appreciatively.

"Bravo, Bravo!" rang out in Judah Benjamin's operatic basso profundo voice as he applauded with exuberance. He adored Varina and she him, not romantically, for their intellectual gifts, cultural interests and all round charm and personalities. But they shared something else. A something that must be guarded from vulgar gaze, the press, the politicians, the generals and the electorate. Jefferson Davis suffered recurring episodes of a sporadic, incapacitating infirmity of unknown etiology that caused severe intractable headache, lens ulceration, and loss of vision in his left eye, ague, chills and fever that could render the

President bedfast and moribund for days and on occasion for a full week. It was then that Varina and Judah, cared for the ailing Davis in camera and essentially ran the government.

As they adjourned the dining room, they both turned to each other as if on signal, Davis spoke first so Benjamin held his tongue. “I’ve been thinking about the subject of our discussion this morning and we should talk.”

“I too have been thinking about the same subject your Excellency and am absolute in my desire to hear your thoughts and have the honor and privilege of sharing my thoughts with you,” replied Benjamin.

“I would be pleased to have you accompany me on my ride out to Tredegar Works this afternoon, just you and I, no aide or attendant and no note taking during or after our carriage talk.” Davis looked to Benjamin who was smiling broadly. “Excellency, I am honored by your kind offer and will honor your demand for the sub rosa status. When do we leave sir?”

The Streets of Richmond VA August 1861

To the eye, it was a beautiful sunny August day in Richmond but other senses perceived the uncomfortable closeness of the prevailing heat and humidity. The slight breeze off the James River provided little relief, in fact it seemed to intensify the discomfort. Adding to this was the aroma from the steady stream of waste being discharged into the James River by the Tredegar Iron Works on its banks. The streets were busy and dusty with traffic of all sorts, civilian, commercial, military, pedestrians, many in uniform, horses, an occasional mule, carriages, carts, wagons, caissons, cannons, ambulances and one hearse. "With all this activity one would think we're at war," observed the President. Benjamin nodded in amused agreement. The ride out was for Davis, the ride back was Benjamin's. Once business was done at the mill and the two were opposite each other in the carriage, Judah lost no time. He started his discourse stating that the President and he were both of the same thought regarding McClellan and the possible opportunity that he could provide invaluable service to his Confederate brethren...to preserve the limbs and lives of his revered classmates and former cadets, their families and fellow citizens, to prevent the devastation of our land and destruction and disappearance of our way of life. He went on to note that this matter was most secret and no official note should be taken or file opened and only Davis and Benjamin should be aware of the subject, at least for the present. Judah Benjamin would be the action officer but Davis must be kept up to date on developments and would be the sole authority to approve or disapprove any action considered, planned, executed or cancelled. Funding would be provided by unaudited and unidentified sources approved only by the President or his appropriately certified and designated agent.

Probing Pasts

Among his other pressing duties required of a Cabinet Officer, of which there was a flood, he was transitioning from Attorney General to Secretary of War at that time. He undertook an in-depth study of General McClellan, who hereafter, in any discussion of this project, will only be referred to as "The Target." It was no small effort in time and was labor intensive for multiple operatives of Benjamin to rifle through Department of Army and other government agency files and civil records surreptitiously. Also many confidential interviews were conducted of acquaintances, employees, and classmates, only southern boys, from his days at West Point to the present. His army days, Mexican War days, bout of malaria, civilian employment, writings, travels, home life, friends, re-enlistment and history of his western Virginia military escapades and loves of his life as well as those of his wife, before but also after their marriage. All were probed discreetly. His present daily activities were being monitored and recorded by observers who were Washingtonians sympathetic to the Confederacy. They reported to Benjamin's agents on a weekly basis and friendlies within the War Department provided copies of the general's orders, plans, schedules and travels. The new Secretary of War was quite proud of the sophistication, complexity and intricacy of his plan...to think it was all of his own; he designed, directed it and enjoyed it. His baptism into the realm of the spymaster was complete and he smiled.

A complete and accurate evaluation entailing mental and physical, financial, spiritual and political aspects of the Target was required to determine if an effective, clandestine, safe approach and recruitment was feasible. And if successful, whether or not assurance of continuous material collection, safe and timely communication and delivery of the work product could be obtained. Absolute secrecy must be maintained absolutely. Accessibility of the Target to available safe and effective means of communication was essential in view of Target's potential transfer to various places. An emergency signal system must be in place so Base-to-Target communication can be accomplished in a safe and timely manner. The use or need for a courier service is to be determined prior to launch date. The use of telegraph is absolutely prohibited.

Benjamin spent sleepless nights fretting over these and many other factors but his main concern was who would make the approach to McClellan or would it take more than one visit? And who would be the courier(s) between him, the Target and Judah Benjamin, the Base?

Despite the increase in demand of time and effort for the success of the Target plan, sandwiched in between a marked increase in the regular required duties of the Secretary of War of a country at war, Judah Benjamin enjoyed a hidden delight and fed a suppressed desire to work. It was play to him, this underworld of the arcane and the surreptitious. Espionage was a challenging art, practiced by a gifted few whose dissembling provided the desired results by using clandestine means and superior intellect. It was human chess in 3 dimensions. The silent world was their domain. Judah eschewed the terms of spy or spying although that's what most would call it. Rather he preferred agent or operator and informant or observer depending upon the specific activity or role. He considered himself to Davis as Sir Francis Walsingham was to Queen Elizabeth the First.

Although he expressed and demonstrated complete loyalty to his President, he knew there was a distinct but unmentioned difference between the two men. Jefferson Davis was a tough West Point trained, decorated combat soldier, then a Mississippi farmer-politician whose intellect was evident in his oratory; clear, to the point, and unfettered by fanciful verbiage. Whereas Judah Benjamin was a genteel, classically educated, astute lawyer, wealthy landowner, successful politician, polished and urbane with the well deserved reputation of being the finest orator of the United States Senate. Yet their similarities were apparent. They were both ambitious, intelligent, capable, determined and energetic in attaining their goals and they both carried grudges. In fact, in response to a verbal affront by Jefferson Davis on the floor of the U.S. Senate in 1858, Judah Benjamin challenged him to a duel. It was rescinded after Davis apologized to Benjamin and the bitterness abated over time and event. A mutuality which grew into admiration and respect was struck between the two. Yet there was still a divide that ran deep and silent.

It was this deep divide that bothered Benjamin when he had to bring his President up to date on the developments of the non-existent project without a name or note. Everything pointed to separating the President from any line of attachment to this project in case this whole affair blew up and got exposed. For his own political future and the preservation of the integrity of the office of the President as strengths in negotiating points, should the opportunity of negotiation occur, lack of any knowledge of such an intelligence operation was an absolute. Davis must be kept in the dark. This was entirely in Judah Benjamin's hands; he would have full responsibility for the affair. Jefferson Davis must not know anything about the Target and plans to recruit and use him. "He won't like it at all and may disallow Plan Target," worried Benjamin out loud, inadvertently christening it a real name, "Plan Target."

The Second Floor Office of the "Gray House"

Jefferson Davis expressed little interest in this matter although he also spent many sleepless nights pondering the many thoughts and worries that war time Presidents endure; occasionally included was Benjamin's Target problem. He knew that Judah was up to it and was pursuing it because he knew that Judah Benjamin loved the idea from the outset. He thought he could see the twinkle in the War Secretary's eye when he first told the story of McClellan. One of these days, Benjamin would be coming to him for approval of a move of some kind. Time will tell.

That time came and Judah Benjamin had prepared for the event as if he were delivering a summation for the defense in a murder trial. Was the jury ready for the event and willing to make the appropriate hoped for verdict? The Secretary was optimistic. His strategy, in the initial part of his exposition was to paraphrase a quotation of Dr. Samuel Johnson, that respected master of the English Language, "It is insufficiently understood that men more frequently need to be reminded than informed." Thus he was not to correct the President concerning his prior inaccurate testimony about George McClellan, the cadet, the soldier and the railroad executive and Nelly's husband. Rather he'd remind Davis of some events of times past that were of such minor import that their exact details were dimmed and distorted by the memories of more current times and events of greater import.

Then Judah Benjamin, the progenitor of "Plan Target," launched into his discourse of how the protagonist of that operation, Major

General George Brinton McClellan, whose code name to be used from that moment on was, "Le Clarion D'argent," which translates in English to," The Silver Bugle." The Target's new name is in French because all communication, verbal and written, between the Base and Target will be in French, since each is French-fluent. The official and final approach for recruitment, Benjamin had finally determined, will be made by the controlling member, Base, "I your Excellency." This meeting will take place in the Target's headquarters city. It would be impossible for the Target to cross lines without an invading army. Whereas the Base, in disguise and with creative means and able accomplices, could cross the line going north and returning south after the meeting with little chance of discovery. Preparations will be made prior to the official approach to soften the Target through his wife and his best friend. The Base will brief Col. Hill and he will brief Nelly. They have maintained a conspiratorial affair though both are married to others. Nelly McClellan and George McClellan are almost strangers living under the same roof with a workable relationship. She likes the socialite lifestyle and pomp and circumstance of a high ranking military wife, and he enjoys the convenience of a spouse on his arm at important business affairs and an attractive hostess at the many house parties. Hill, who is presently serving as the Colonel of the 13th Virginia Volunteers, will also contact the Target to lend weight to the argument that supports the recruitment. Both Nelly and Hill will be briefed on ways to provide convincing arguments to the Target to assure his agreement to meet with the person in the official approach.

At this point, Benjamin revealed to Davis that detailed extensive detective work had been accomplished. This work provided personal profiles of the potential participants. It was determined that the necessary ethical and moral standards and political convictions of the selectees were in accord with the rationale, objectives and operation of the mission and would comply with its required actions. Following this investigation, it was concluded with a reasonable degree of certainty that the selectees met and would affirm the above stated requirements. Of interest is that no financial reward was proffered or sought. The identity of the party conducting the official approach was not revealed. The entire operation and those involved, directly or indirectly, are cloaked in the utmost secrecy and must not communicate any knowledge of the plan, its existence, activity or those involved.

Davis was falling asleep, he had not been well for a few days. He left his chair, extended his hand to Benjamin and said, "my congratulations, you work miracles while others moan and groan about seniority and lack of appropriate uniforms. When will your plan be functional?"

"There is no launch date set, sir," answered Benjamin.

"Keep up the good work. You have my approval to carry on as you see fit. Good luck and God speed. I'm going to bed." With that the ailing President shuffled out of the room.

Plan Target was to proceed unencumbered and the Silver Bugle was in waiting, unaware.

A Campsite of The Army of Northern Virginia South of Manassas, Virginia

"Colonel sir, a courier from Richmond has just arrived with a sealed message marked for most urgent direct delivery for you alone." A. P. Hill's orderly stood in the tent's entrance alongside a dust covered, sweat soaked soldier who appeared trail weary. Salutes were exchanged and the rider stepped forward, "My orders are, sir, to deliver this dispatch to the hand of Col. Ambrose Powell Hill only."

"I am he and here is my hand," Hill extended his hand, approached the courier and took possession of the sealed envelope. "Thank you. When did you eat or sleep last cause boy you look hungry and beat tired?"

Ambrose Powell Hill, Colonel commanding of the 13th Virginia Volunteers, superb horseman, gifted leader of men, 5'10" tall, 155 lbs., narrow of chest and shoulders, high cheek bones, chiseled nose. His pale skin accentuated the red tinge of his mustache matching a full head of curls above blue-gray eyes. A genial exterior hid a smoldering sensitivity and nervous volatile nature, quick to take offense...he was a soldier by birth and training.

"Corporal," he turned to his orderly, "get this gentleman some real food and a place to rest his weary bones for a spell. And by the way," he smiled, "congratulations on your second stripe...you well deserved it. Now take this soldier to some comfort and let me get to this most urgent thing." They saluted, departed and Hill sat at his camp desk, unsealed the envelope, unfolded a one page document with the letterhead of The Secretary of War of The Confederate States of America. Surprised, actually stunned by the letterhead, he read the message, only 3 sentences, signed by the adjutant to the Secretary, frowned at its contents and murmured, "What in damnation requires my unaccompanied presence at the War Department in Richmond 'as soon as conveyance can be arranged'...what do I do now?"

Richmond was a good day's ride from the camp so he made haste in arranging command and staff matters, collected his gear, fed and watered his horse, Champ, a steel-gray mount, and set off. There was a storm in his brain of thoughts for questions to answer because there was no obvious question to answer or pending problem to solve that would have the purview of the Secretary of War, the Honorable Judah P. Benjamin. This was his brain's conclusion of the mental storm. Despite this no-answer answer, he ruminated over recent and remote, civilian and military actions, deeds, events, happenings, statements, writings...but nothing made sense. "Oh well," he thought, "time will tell." On he rode... still ruminating.

Void of logical reasons to explain his sudden obligatory visit to Secretary Benjamin, he forced his mind to address other topics. He reminisced of his halcyon days at West Point and his friends and cohorts, some now enemies, in name only---how strange and uncomfortable for all of us. His young lady friends, on and off post, came into mind and, of course, dear sweet Nel, love of loves, was at the top of that list...no need or desire to look farther than her. His heart and mind wouldn't allow it. That love burned bright in the depth of his being and nothing would extinguish that flame. And she suffered that same pain of separation...she told him many times as she lay in his arms in all of their clandestine trysts. He reined in Champ to a halt and sat there pondering the many what-ifs. Those trysts were cut off when Nel's men went to war. How sweet those times were and how convenient it was that Mac was required to be off on railroad business frequently and occasionally for extended periods. Nel had made a great new friend, Abigail Wallingford, in Cincinnati, where Nel and Mac had settled after his appointment to head the railroad.

Hill smiled and recalled when Nel found out she was moving to Cincinnati, she looked at the map to see how much closer she and I would be and she was very pleased. She lost no time and spared no energy to establish herself among the Cincinnati social whirlpool. The main swimmer in that pool of social elites was Abigail Wallingford. She already knew her from dinners and social functions she attended with the general when he was being courted to be the railroad president. Nelly and Abby, as she preferred to be called by her close friends, clicked when they first met and, with a method to her madness, Nel generated an intimacy with Abby. They shared secrets with one another---deep secrets.

Abby had married a much older, wealthy businessman and lived on a large estate on the outskirts of the city with well-stocked stables and broad fields for grazing and rolling hills for the hunts. There were well-maintained horse paths through the woods and a lovely guest cottage tucked away in the privacy of a stand of tall pines a respectable distance from the mansion. This cottage served the purposes of just a few guests. Abby's husband also had to be away on business more than he would like so Abby made the most of it by using it as a love nest for her paramour who was the Master of the Hunt. Abby shared her secrets with Nelly who confided in Abby her own affair. The seed was planted, so between the two of them a plan of romantic intrigue blossomed. The guest list of the cottage added two new names and the two new guests afforded themselves loving adventures a number of times. An active correspondence had been in place for quite awhile between A.P. and Nelly. With new arrangements, Hill would post letters to Nelly addressed to Abigail's country estate and she would post hers to his headquarters address. But that was prewar and things had changed markedly since the firing on Fort Sumter. Time to make necessary modifications in visitation plans; correspondence, thankfully was unchanged.

Champ neighed and bucked his head a couple of times. “OK old boy,” Hill responded, “I guess it’s time to move on.” He started a canter for a short while then brought the horse to a walk....still ruminating. This time he thought of his wife whom he also loved but it was a different kind of love. Dolly was a good wife and mother and loyal---she’d be heart broken if she ever discovered the secret off-and-on affair that Nel and I share.

There’s Nel again, I can’t help it. In fact I’m overdue in making contact with her especially since fast and furious Mac is moving up so rapidly in the world. Who would have known? Good old Mac, maestro supremo of wherever he finds himself or whatever he makes himself. He too would be devastated if he ever found out about Nelly and me....or would he? From what Nel tells me he already has made some strange and vapid comments occasionally without addressing the issue directly in a tone that almost is accepting.

Richmond, Virginia, November 1861

There was a chill in the air but nothing like the chill running up Hill's spine as he rode up crowded streets to the state capitol, now the capitol of the Confederate States of America. He spent the night before at an inn just outside the city limits because there was no room at three hostels in the city. As it was, he had to share the two bed room with three others who were civilians on government business or trying to be.

There was two-way traffic on the steps of the capitol building, everyone was in a hurry with a rare smile among a majority wearing a look of grave concern. Breaking loose from those with the grave looks, Hill forced a smile and rode Champ up to a standing uniformed sentry who presented arms recognizing the approach of a field grade officer on horseback. Hill returned the salute with an "at rest soldier" and remarked how smart the sentry appeared. "Where's the War Department located?" The sentry looked Hill in the eye and said, "Sir I don't even know where the latrine is. You might try askin somebody inside." The trooper then approached Champ took his bridle and was given the reins as Hill dismounted. "Thank you Trooper, I'll be back as soon as I find out where I'm going." And up the steps he scrambled two at a time. Moments later he was hopping down the steps, mounted his horse and galloped away to 9th street where the Virginia Mechanics Institute housed the Department of Justice of the Confederate States of America, (the first department of justice in America; it preceded the United States Department of Justice by 7 months). Judah Philip Benjamin was the Attorney

General and was the engineer who organized this revolutionary department into the well-oiled and effective legal machinery of the confederacy's government. That was in early 1861. Then in September of 1861, he was appointed Secretary of War with offices in the same building so he didn't have much of a moving bill. And that's where "little Powell," as he was known as a youngster, was headed apprehensively, feeling just like that youngster, into the great unknown. "Oh well," he said aloud, "time will tell."

Arriving in a room too small for the array of stuff and people occupying it, he found himself amid stacks of books, piles of papers, partially unpacked boxes and scurrying people. Almost no one was sitting at a desk because there were only a few of them and the only chairs, other than those at the desks, were placed at two large map covered conference tables. Hovered over the tables were uniformed officers pointing and conversing with no small measure of passion. The clerk who was called to the guard desk to escort him to Secretary Benjamin's office, marched through the center of this commotion and past one desk occupied by a young enlisted man just outside a closed, solid dark-paneled door. The desk holder looked up, nodded and went back to his papers. The escort knocked three times opened the door ajar and announced his arrival, "Mr. Secretary, Colonel Hill has arrived."

"And in one fine looking solid piece I am delighted and pleased to see but most honoured that you have given of your most valued time, compelling requirements of command and suffered the awful discomforts of the journey to grace these primitive settings. I am most grateful to you sir." And that's how the brilliant, distinguished, famous Secretary of War of the Confederate States of America, Judah Philip Benjamin greeted Little Powell Hill.

Short, stout, a full head of black hair, thin chin line beard under an oval face, thin lips locked in a perpetual smile that softened the black penetrating beady eyes resting under generous eyebrows, impeccably dressed, the Honorable Mr. Benjamin extended his soft, puffy right hand with stubby fingers to officially welcome A.P. Hill. A.P. saluted, shook the Secretary's extended hand and responded, "Mr. Secretary it is a great honour and pleasure to meet you but I am of much angst as to the reason of your order for my presence." He continued, "If sir........" Benjamin interrupted, waved his chubby hand, emitted a short chuckle and said, "My dear Colonel, you may rest assured that my request for your presence was for no other purpose than to beg of your most desired and required assistance, of which only you can render, in developing plans of an operation of the highest strategic importance to this Confederacy's enduring independence, prosperity...and yes, Colonel, our survival. You, kind sir, among all your other accomplishments, attributes qualities and talents, have a most unique gift....that gift is the mutual love, respect and trust of the enduring intimate friendship enjoyed by you and your old West Point roommate, George Brinton McClellan."

A short silent pause befell the stark chamber. Benjamin moved to the door, opened it, nodded to his orderly, closed the door and moved to the center of the room, looked directly at Hill and said, " We need you both and we need you now."

Hill was still standing staring straight ahead, moving no muscle and silent. At that point the door opened and the orderly brought in a large silver tray, set it on the side board and left. No word spoken only slight nods given and received by the Secretary and his aide.

Tea and crumpets were in evidence and two brandy snifters were in place, on a sideboard, ceremoniously guarding each side of a crystal decanter of golden brandy. Pointing to the display with an open palm, Benjamin suggested "a little something" to ease the burden of the journey, pointed to a Hitchcock chair with arms and said, "Please sit, make yourself comfortable. We're going to be here for a good while talking about something of the greatest importance to our country as I just mentioned-----its survival.

And you my dear Colonel, will enjoy a major role in this endeavor. You will be, no, you are the decisive player, the protagonist in this drama of destiny." He smiled and sat in a matching chair slightly angled toward Hill's.

In the pregnant silence that followed his ice-breaking introduction, the Secretary went to the sideboard and poured more than two swallows worth of brandy in each snifter. He offered one to Hill, sat and lifted his snifter, toward the Colonel, "a toast to our good, happy, healthy, long and prosperous lives, and to the everlasting glory of our country." Hill picked up his snifter, tapped his to Benjamin's, heard the crystal sing, "Hear hear," exhorted Hill and they both took a swallow. Hill's was a tad bit more generous than his host.

"What is this drama of destiny in which I have such an important role?" asked A.P. Judah took in a deep breath left his chair and looked sternly at Hill.

"Before we proceed in our discussion I must ask of you, demand of you, complete secrecy of anything and everything we discuss. You may not even tell Dolly, your wife or your priest." At the mention of Dolly, Benjamin noted a slight start in Hill. "Oh yes," he said, as he tilted his head and shifted his eyes in a conspiratorial way, "my investigations left no stone unturned, you see Colonel, this mission is of such gravity, magnitude and sensitivity that we must go to the ends of the earth to guard its secrets. Justified thusly, the breadth and depth of my investigation which revealed, as one would expect, some extremely delicate personal matters."......... Benjamin paused for effect, smiled and said, "yes, matters that, were they to become unveiled, would be catastrophic for the involved individuals legally, socially, politically and, yes maritally. I know you well Colonel and what I know I like....and I will protect your secrets because they are now our secrets with my final earthly breath.Your affair with Nelly is an essential part of the plan."

Benjamin poured more brandy into the snifters, lifted his and exclaimed, "sounds interesting doesn't it. but what say you?" as he reached for a document on his desk and read from it, "do I have your sworn oath that on the threat of death you will not discuss, divulge or reveal any act, device, document, event, person, place, thought or word that pertains to this project directly or indirectly to anyone who is not personally project-authorized by President Jefferson Davis or Secretary Judah Benjanin. Sworn and signed by me, Ambrose Powell Hill, Col., C.S.A. on this blank day blank month, 1861?"

Hill took another slug of the brandy, rose to his feet, almost at attention. He stared at Benjamin with a mixed expression of disdain and disbelief, paused, took another swallow of brandy, emptied his snifter, reached over, grabbed the decantrer and poured 3 finger breadths of the liquor into each snifter.

"Before I swear an oath for anybody or for any reason," he started, "I must know a hell of a lot more than what you've told me, time to think about it, and be damn sure what I'm swearing to is right and doable." He drank 2 finger breadths of the brandy and said," Sir, I'm here under your orders and I must obey them and will, but I need some brains and guts instead of straw to make this scarecrow somebody or some meat to put on the bones of this skeleton. Please sir, I'm a simple soldier, help me so I can help you." At that he sat, all eyes and ears at the ready.

The Secretary, smiled, took a sip of brandy, walked to the window, turned and motioned for Hill to join him. "Look out there," directed the Secretary, "what do you see? You see the spires of cathedrals, the bell towers of all faiths, the temples of healing, the domes of insitutes of learning, the smokestacks of industries, the buildings of commerce, the markets of the farm, the museums of art and history, the concert halls and theaters, the hallowed halls of government, the railroad locomotives and steamboats, and finally the chimneys and rooftops under which our fine fellow citizens live and breed. This my dear Colonel is the land we love, where we live and thrive and raise our treasured families with plans for their perpetuity. But all that is threatened....threatened I say." Benjamin stood back from the window, his operatic basso profundo voice filling the room, his eyes glistened. In silence, he thrust his right fist in the air, then by reducing the meter of his delivery by pronouncing each word slowly and accentuating key syllables, broke the silence with, "Our murderous invaders, in overwhelming numbers, with unlimited resouces, a surplus in treasure and insatiable lust, as we speak, are forming to crash our gates and arming to crush our people, to plague our waters, lay waste our fields and annihilate our culture. Armageddon is here.

But there is hope and you, kind sir, are chosen by God to be the messenger to deliver that gift of hope! To preserve our land, to perpetuate our society, to save our people and a future for our progeny ...you have the key."

Hill was beside himself. He was still and listened intently while Benjamin was preaching but when he stopped, Hill shifted about the room, hands clasped behind his back, head down obviously in deep thought. He turned, faced his host and almost pleading said,"But tell me how. How is this poor ground-pounding soldier gonna save the Confederacy? I sure don't know how," turning his head from side-to-side in the movement in body language that signals a negative reaction.

The clock on the mantlepiece chimed noon and afforded Benjamin the opportunity to break the tension. "Alas, the blessed timepiece announces a reprieve from the travails of our world. Let us afford our minds and bodies some nourishment. That old clock is from France and its chime songs, beautiful are they not, are those of the Cathedral of Notre Dame in Paris." He went to the wall behind his desk and gave three pulls on the bell cord and in moments the office door opened revealing his orderly pushing a linen-covered food cart to the center of the room. He elevated both leaves and set places for two. "As ordered, sir, " he said, "luncheon was delivered by noon and the hot items are still hot." He then placed two chairs on either side of the cart, stepped to the back of one chair and waited to seat the Secretary.

"Come now Colonel, we'd best avail ourselves of this bounty, I have a new cook and she is a goddess of culinary arts. Be that as it may, I've requested light fare for us." Benjamin sat and his chair was adjusted by his orderly. Hill had already seated himself before the orderly could get to his chair. A baked ham adorned with candied cherries, pineapple slices and christened with raisin sauce was already stacked in manageable individiual portions on a silver platter. Buttered string beans and au gratin potatoes were the vegetables and warm buttered corn bread in cubes lay in wait in a silver wire bread basket. A decanter of white wine was the centerpiece of the table. A silver tea service was placed on the sideboard. "Bon appetite, mon amis," Benjamin added, "I trust this is a welcome relief from your field mess."

"Most certainly," responded Hill "and most appreciated." The orderly poured the wine then Judah Benjamin thanked him for his service, requested not to be disturbed and dismissed him. When the door latch clicked, Benjamin turned to Hill and said,"now Colonel Hill, to the heart of the matter and once again I don't request but I must demand your oath of allegiance and secrecy for what you are about to hear and know, no matter your decision to cooperate or not cooperate once you've been fully informed of the project and its absolute need for you absolutely."

A.P. shifted uncomfortably in his chair. "Please sir," plead his Secretary, "I can wait no longer before I order you, by the authority of the President, to comply with my demand."

"In that case I have no choice,,,,,,so Mr. Secretary, you have my sworn oath"....as he was talking, Benjamin reached for the document and pen and thrust them in front of A.P. Hill....."and

I will sign it and find out if I have just signed my life away." So he signed the document and was immediately embraced by Benjamin. "And now kind sir, please elucidate my requirements and actions my role entails," said Hill with almost a note of relief in his voice. The window dressing was no longer required, the preliminaries were over. It was time to get the real story. And he was ready and so was Benjamin.

THE PLAY AND THE PLAYERS

The session lasted a little over three hours. Judah Benjamin delivered a complete presentation of Plan Target and the Silver Bugle, perhaps for the first time ever, without the flourish of oratory and grandiosity of performace for which he was noted on the floor of the Senate. He was concise, precise and to the point, more like Jefferson Davis than Judah Benjamin. But the job was done. The Colonel's reactions to the information imparted and received were multiple and varied and changed as he was piloted through the shadowed paths of intrigue and subterfuge. Amazed, apprehensive, humbled and honored. He was each of these at one or more points but finally he was committed. And Judah Benjamin rejoiced aloud and once again embraced A.P. Hill. "Colonel, I must go now but I assure you for a very short time and deliver this glorious gift to the President in person, no despatch by courier, nothing in writing. I will show him your signed oath but will maintain its possession and safeguard it. And I will return and take you to my home to meet young lovely Jules St Martin, my brother-in-law and an actor in our drama. Remember he will be the recipient of correspondence from Nelly through Mrs. Wallingford and hand carry it to me and will post my returns. He lives with me."

Hill had no receptive expression on his face when he said," Mr. Secretary, I offer my most humble and sincere appreciaton for your gracious invitation but unhappily I must tender my regrets. Duty calls and I must return to my command."

"Colonel, I am your Secretay of War and am changing my invitation to an order."

"Yes sir." An automatic reply in a parade ground voice and Hill sat'

I am a gourmet chef and will prepare for you a sumptuous repast optimized by a fine French wine. Then we will retire to the drawing room for brandy, cigars and stimulating conversation. You'll find Jules charming and I'm certain he will find you fascinating. Then you may grace our guest room for a pleasant slumber to be well-rested for your day's journey after a wholesome Virginia country breakfast, of course. In the meantime, please make yourself comfortable, ask the orderly for anything you need. Think over what we just discussed and develop a plan of action. We will address any concerns on my return," and he left.

Alone in this cold cavern, the silence broken only by the ticking of the mantle clock and its quarterly chimes, Hill looked over the room, perhaps for the first time. The window panes were smoke streaked with no curtain or shade. The fireplace, shoulder height tall, had charred log remnants resting in blackened cannonball andirons from many fires past. The floor was pine darkened with age, unpolished for years with no carpet. The woodwork about the room was once white except the door which was dark-paneled. The desk and chair appeared to be government issue. The two wingbacks by the fireplace were worn and every flat surface was covered with papers, loose sheets and stacks of books, some open and maps, rolled, folded and open. Hill paced slowly collecting his thoughts about the vagaries and various stages of Plan Target, learning and using secret ink technology and sharing the knowledge with Nelly. In fact, the whole business involving Nelly would be challenging, like finding the time for a visit to Abigail's cottage to introduce Nelly to Plan Target, get her acceptance of the rationale and workability of the plan, commitment to its operational requirements, maintaining absolute secrecy and assuring continuing success of the mission. She's an intelligent and savvy girl, she'll catch on fast. And if she is convinced, she should have no trouble convincing George to render God's will through George's humble efforts to assist in the cause of peace.

She knows him better than he knows himself. She'll be able to play to his inflated self image, his driving ambition, his lust for power and his thin skin....she's done it for sometime. That brings me to the George meeting. The meeting of the two of us will be a real challenege. the place, the time and duration. Where, when and how are the difficulties, the 'what' is easy. We're still close fiends, not as close as he thinks because he tells me everything and confides in me matters that he doesn't share with his wife. I know because she tells me so. So a channel of communication between us is active now via the post. And he knows that I know his political inclinations and sincere southern sympathy. So. as I see it and as I've told Mr. Benjamin, appealing to his overly ambitious nature, insatiable appetite for greatness and his desire to be number one would almost guarantee his seeing the light and accepting his God-given mission of helping to secure a lasting peace.

And Nelly, she would be agreeable to the plan and her vital role in it. Furthermore she would have no trounble in preparing the court for our critical game of croquet by referring to and discussing my letter frequently prior to my visit. She most likely will happily concentrate on his potential for a grander future to include the presidency of the United States of America. She'd love that... First Lady. At this thought he developed a mischievous grin then laughed out loud.

There was a noise in the outer office and in burst the Secretary of War.

Judah Benjamin had a noticeable bounce to his gait, the only visble indication that things went well, because his perpetual half smile trademark was unchanged. "The President was not well at all when I arrived but the news I gave him brought some comfort and cheer to his misery," the Secretary reported.

Hill smiled and said, "That is excellent Mr. Secretary and I am pleased and honoured to know my small contribution to the cause was salubrious for Mr. Davis." Benjamin went to the door, opened it and said,"Shall we go home? It is a pleasant walk" And out they went for a pleasant walk to the Davenport house on Main street.

Dinner At the Davenport House

Hill would rather be in camp at mess with his staff. He had had enough of Richmond's rat race but orders are just that, so obey he does. Insubordination is not one of the arrows in Hill's quiver of military do's. There was little conversation between the two during their walk to Main Street. Benjamin was used to ambling along with his short choppy gait holding his silver-tipped ebony walking stick in his soft puffy hand with stubby fingers, greeting passersby and tipping his hat to the ladies, after all he was still a politician and always on the campaign trail. But keeping pace with the Colonel's military stride caused him an increase in breaths and steps per minute. He was puffing by the time they reached his home. During the welcome silence of the walk, Hill contrived a justification for this interruption in his own plans to return to his troops, his boys. At least I'll learn more about Judah Benjamin, the devil's genius behind the plan. The more I know about the man who has the power of life and death over me the better I will be.

His makeshift office in the rented Mechanic's Institute was sparsely furnished with government issue utilitarian pieces that told little of its occupant. The color gray and two dimensions were conjured by the brain that formed its mental picture of the place. Surely his living quarters will give color and depth to the man whom I must obey, respect, serve and hopefully admire and please and trust. And I will meet a close member of his immediate family, the bed and board are the least of the benefits.

Jules St. Martin, his brother-in-law, greeted Judah by an embrace as if they hadn't seen each other in months with a few soft spoken words in Judah's ear in French. Upon his release, Judah turned and introduced the guest to Jules who emitted a warm smile, bowed and welcomed him. Hill returned the bow and expressed his pleasure in meeting him and being their guest. They were ushered into the parlor, Jules, acting as host, offered Hill one of the wing backs at either side of the fireplace and the Secretary took the other. Jules spoke to Benjamin in French and was immediately interrupted by his brother-in-law who said, " Please my dear Jules, only English this evening." "But of course, as you desire." replied Jules in English.

The house was the antithesis to the office. High ceilings with sculpted cornices, sprouting multi-tiered crystal chandeliers and paneled walls, some painted ivory, some stained oak with gilt- framed wall hangings of varied heredities, looked down on floors covered by multiple multi-colored and patterned oriental carpets. Window treatments were in chintz and most furnishings were Louis Quatorze. A few gilt-edge paged and titled leather-bound tomes rested comfortably on some end tables and in the drawing room. Hill never saw the library. Benjamin's homestead exuded opulent wealth. From what was said by the hosts, their not infrequent receptions celebrated in the Davenport house were the favorites of the local dignitaries, government officials and foreign diplomats.

Hill found Jules an interesting study. Rumors, in some circles, had it that he was Judah's lover. He was long of limb and thin, frail, fine featured, almost gaunt, of sallow complexion, high cheekbones, deeply-set dark eyes, Gallic nose, beardless, shoulder length brown hair, hands of a woman with well bitten nails, gaze well focused when attending a person or thing or Benjamin but most often oft to infinity. He was outfitted in the fashion of the European dignitaries and diplomats that Hill saw at the embassy parties when he worked for Jefferson Davis in Washington. Jules' cologne competed with the slight aroma of incense apparent upon entering the home. His demeanor was refined, the etiquette of the well-bred, his mannerisms slightly effeminate and he appeared to be a boy of late teens yet stated to be in the early thirties. He was most attentive to his brother-in-law but denied no measure of courtesy or hospitality to Hill. He served the table in food and was the sommelier of wine. The table was set with a silver service, Limoges china and Irish crystal resting on damask linen. The fare was a veal flambe of some sort, it had a French name, with potatoes au gratin, spinach souffle and strawberries in cream for dessert. A fine French white wine was decanted by Jules who allowed no vessel to be less than half full. Conversation centered around a number of very old volumes of poetry that the two had bought in Europe and sent here. There was a great delay in getting the books to Richmond but they had arrived a few days before and Jules and Judah were reading them aloud to each other. Politics, the war and the Plan were not mentioned.

Hill excused himself early, citing the exhausting day, and retired to the well appointed guest room for a much needed slumber. Before he slept he penned a brief note to Nelly citing the absolute need for an urgent rendezvous to discuss a most important matter. "With all my love, respond immediately," was its ending. It was a deep and restful sleep, enhanced by one pleasant dream of Nelly. They loved and laughed and languished for each other in Abigail's sunlit cottage in the pines. He awoke refreshed, had a good breakfast, said his thanks to his hosts and was on his way back to his men on good old Champ. The first stop was the post office to send Nelly's note.

Preparing For The Target

Judah Benjamin lost no time in making the necessary preparations. He sent written instructions for using secret inks to Hill, even though A.P. had been tutored in the use of secret writing during his Richmond visit. He was to train Nelly and she to train her husband in secret writing.

Judah Benjamin decided not to use hard to acquire chemicals, the agent, the invisible ink and the reagent, the chemical to make the written message reappear. Rather, he planned on using readily available agents and reagents. Equal parts of baking soda and water for the invisible ink and purple grape juice or heat for the reagent. There were many more sophisticated methods of producing invisible ink and of remaking the product visible but they required the use of chemical agents that would be unavailable in the field and raise eyebrows of suspicion when sought after on the civilian market. Simplicity was sensibility and simplicity ensured security and success.

The line of secret communication would be from the Target to Nelly, from Nelly to Abigail, from her to Jules to Benjamin. Return messages would use the same pathway in reverse. Only the Target and Base would use the secret ink to write and read the secret writing. At the end of every run all correspondence was to be burned by the end user or addressee. Absolute secrecy was a must and if so maintained the network was foolproof. Talking points for Hill and Nelly for discussions with the Silver Bugle were composed and sent to Hill, with the usual post-read-burn rule. A scenario was planned to execute the face-to-face approach and recruit meeting between the Target and Base in Alexandria so the

Bugle need not leave his headquarters area. Arrangements with an Alexandria dentist who was a Confederate spy were underway. The Bugle would develop a toothache on schedule to be treated by that dentist in his Alexandria office where the approach and recruitment will be executed. Once the Bugle is recruited, he will be instructed in secret writing so he can insert his reports in Nelly's letters and receive requirements from Base.

Benjamin thought long and hard over who should be the agent of approach and recruitment eventually coming to the conclusion that only he should be that person, dangerous as it may be. And Davis should not be informed of this decision until after the fact because he would deny permission for such action. Benjamin could hear in his mind the arguments negating his being the agent to recruit the Bugle face-to-face in the headquarters of the enemy. " How dare you cause me such vexation! You, my most trusted and valued member of the Cabinet exposing our country to ruination by such insanity, such mindless thought and behavior! Only in your wildest nightmare could you concoct such a morbid plan.-----How would you get across the picket line once let alone twice undetected?---If, not when, you got captured, you'd be jailed, tried as a spy and executed----What would we do without you?---The Confederacy would collapse---Who would run that awful stable of miscreants, smugglers and thugs you call spies----Who would invent, develop and operate our secret services here and abroad?----Who would be able to replace you for the services you render me legally, professionally, politically, and personally?----you are the brains of the Confederacy, the soul of the movement." These and other points of contention would be brought up, doom and gloom would prevail. Varina would hang funeral crepe about the Gray House..... And invariably, shortly, the word would get out, the mission compromised and I'd be dead on arrival.

So, Benjamin's decision was firm and well founded. He felt that, owing to the Bugle's inflated self image, his elemental conceit and his mental makeup, he would suffer a negative impression to the extreme if a nameless unknown from the shadows of the enemy's espionage bin with no authority, import, or reputation was sent to carry a message from those on high. To be affronted by such an underling would be a colossal insult. So who better to impress, compliment, approach and recruit this savior, our awaiting gift of salvation, than the most revered and honorable Judah Philip Benjamin, former United States Senator from Louisiana, former Attorney General of the Confederate States of America and present Secretary of War of the Confederacy. The act would be played as an encounter of not just man-to-man but genius-to-genius. Benjamin must come off in McClellan's mind, as the brilliant originator and director of this secret visionary operation, as one of the worthy who recognizes McClellan's God-blessed ability to bring peace to our beloved land. The very reputation alone of Benjamin would guarantee at least an audience with the Bugle. And he alone, his brilliance in eloquence of argument and power of persuasion, would be the one most likely to succeed in moving that star into their galaxy.

"You know," he said to himself out loud while viewing his image in a girandole hanging on the wall, "you really are a genius, McClellan and I have much in common, but I am smarter, and I will emphasize our mutual abilities and desires when we meet. Furthermore, I will endeavor to assuage his anxieties and assure his awareness and appreciation of the plan which, on the surface, appears to be a very complex structure requiring many actors and activities vulnerable to the threat of detection. But that's the beauty of it. It is not complex; it is simple and easily workable. Its simplicity negates the threat of detection and failure. There are few actors, all beyond reproach and none of the required activities, properly executed, would arouse any suspicion. Its openness and common acts are its strengths whereas the dark acts by those in shadows are the weaknesses of espionage. The maxim of hidden in plain sight prevails.

ALEXANDRIA, VIRGINIA

Just around the corner from the Mansfield House Hotel, the premier hostelry in Alexandria, Virginia, owned and operated by James Green, a British-born Virginia entrepreneur of strong southern sympathies was the dwelling and operatory of Dr. Aaron Van Camp, a practicing dentist and actual agent of the Confederacy. He was a member of the Greenhow Spy Ring, organized by Captain Thomas Jordan. a West Point graduate working in Washington. Before his resignation from the U.S. Army he organized and recruited spies for the first Confederate spy net in Washington, of which there were at least three. Rose O'Neal Greenhow, famous merry-widow socialite about town, was his first recruit and he made her leader of that ring that remained active and most fruitful following his transfer from D.C. He was commissioned Lt. Colonel on the staff of Confederate General Beauregard.

Washington was abuzz with Confederate sympathizers and spies, espionage was rampant; most of the townies were of southern blood and temperament and were the worker bees for the federal government. They were the permanent residents. Whereas, the elected members of government and their cronies, staff members and lobbyists were out-of-towners, visitors, some not so welcome, not of southern leanings and learnings. And there was no love lost between the two. So the rebel collectors of intelligence had a field day because a military secret in Washington was a joke. Aside from Thomas Jordan's network of spies, couriers and sympathizers, there were at least two other organized espionage networks operating in Washington as well as the many un-numbered freelance operators. The second network was directed by Captain Thomas Nelson Conrad and the third by Benjamin

Franklin "Frank" Stringfellow, both reporting to General J.E.B. Stuart. These two had an undefined connection to the Confederate Signal Service which became the Army Signal Corps in 1862 under Major William Norris. It was essentially an espionage service and clandestine communication system with flag, torch and telegraph signals. Agents and couriers operated in the North, Canada, Bermuda and England. Despite the fact that there was no centralized intelligence service, the tentacles of Confederate intelligence were well in place and functional months before the first shot was fired at Fort Sumter. Once Judah Benjamin was Secretary of War, he became the major domo of all strategic (Richmond originated and operated) espionage and intelligence operations and scarcely a few of the tactical (field military, army scout) operations. The latter groups were run by local army commanders from lieutenants to generals.

Dr. Van Camp was notified by word of mouth that he would soon participate in a most secret and extremely vital meeting in his operatory between parties whose identities and mission are so secret that the threat of death hangs over any who violates his oath of secrecy. He was informed that his role in this operation is absolutely essential, obligatory and he may not refuse his assistance and cooperation by order of the Secretary of War. The matter is of such delicacy that no written order shall appear and Dr. Van Camp was not to divulge to anyone, wife, family, friend or fellow partisan this message, its means of delivery, the sender or the courier. A further message with instructions will be delivered by the same courier and means in a week or two. Dr. Van Camp was given the oath, repeated it, swore to it and signed it. The courier took it before the ink was dry, stuffed it into his boot top, shook Van Camp's hand and said, "Thank you sir, the future of the Confederacy is in your hands," and left. The dentist felt stunned, anxious, a bit light-headed and sat quickly into his dental chair. A slight sweat broke out with a wave of nausea." Dear God," he said, "I must do what I must do. Please help me through this." And he vomited.

THE DAVENPORT HOUSE

"Sometimes my brilliance astounds me...but then, in retrospect, it doesn't. Rather it is to be expected and de rigueur," Judah Benjamin thought out loud and chuckled softly at his self analysis, smiled and turned to his beloved Jules, who was watching, quietly amused. He was the only one with whom Judah could be unguarded in word or deed and they both knew it.

"My dear Jules, my cerebral concoctions will be the death of me and this cunning stratagem may be the one but it is delicious, creative and appeals to my latent thespian desires. If successful---there is no reason to assume it won't be---I will have accomplished a coup de main extraordinaire. I will be the true Messiah of the Confederate States of America---even more so than what I am now." And he gave forth with a staccato of deep hearty laughter that made his generous belly bounce. He embraced Jules then strutted to the center of the parlor and pronounced, "I will enter into the enemy's territory as a portly French Chef who has sampled in excess of his delectable culinary creations. I will be a member of the French Consul General's official party when they travel from Richmond to Washington to greet the French noblemen who will be seconded to the Union Army General Staff as military observers. I will leave the party in Alexandria, accomplish my mission and return with all the comforts of heaven." At this point he burst out laughing until tears came to his eyes. Jules had never seen such a display of joviality. Judah Philip Benjamin almost shouted, "I will return in a coffin!"

Sudden silence, then, startled, with his eyes popping and jaw dropped, Jules leapt to his feet. Obviously shaken, voice cracked, he whimpered, "What are you saying? His words becoming more distinct and louder, he uttered, "Your words and manner are disturbing and frightening. I don't regard this as humour; it is hurtful to hear." His head dropped.

Benjamin eased toward St, Martin, placed a hand on his shoulder and spoke softly. "I beseech you to fret not and be calm. I will explain in due course the sanity and sense of the apparent insane meanderings of my mind." He then proceeded to lay out the details of his plan to recross the lines to safety in Richmond. "I will return disguised as a pox-smitten corpse who is on his way to burial in the grave yard of Saint John's Church in Richmond. I will have a most comfortable journey recumbent on soft silken pillows in a very elaborate and private casket complete with an appropriate stock of food and drink for such a momentous occasion.....and, of course, my funereal chaise lounge will be well-ventilated." He went on to explain that the wagon carrying the casket will be driven by a freed black man who will inform the checkpoint sentries that the man in the coffin died of the pox or plague. The doctor put some kind of a restriction on the body according to the wagon driver, " If yo was a ship yo'd be flyin a yaller flag." Benjamin stage-whispered, " You can rest assured that no self-respecting, life-loving trooper will want to open the coffin to check its human cargo." He chuckled.

Jules forced a smile, strode to the sideboard and poured himself a generous brandy and drank it down without the customary ritual of swirling the brandy in the snifter. He just drank it down in two or three swallows. "Judah, Judah, Judah, oh my dear Judah." he intoned. And he sobbed. Judah put both arms around him squeezed tightly, rocked him and spoke softly in his ear, "My love, things will work well and we, you and I, will celebrate a wondrous outcome."

Benjamin broke away from the embrace, with an element of forced joviality to change Jules' mood. "We must invite Alfred Paul for dinner this week, Friday would be good. We owe him for the last time we dined together, we were his guests. Also I want to make certain the details of our official trip to Washington are in order, the date verified and our portly French Chef is on the travel list. Would you be so kind to visit the Consulate tomorrow to extend the invitation and accept no denial. Please tell the Consul I insist he put all matters of interference aside for I have matters of extreme urgency to impart and discuss. The dinner will be simple, not formal, an intimate family dinner, and we consider Paul family. He will be the only guest and we will serve him the fare of his choice. With his acceptance and his food choice known, please purchase the required items to meet his request. We already know and have his favorite wine. Then, my dear, please demonstrate your well learned culinary skills, that I taught you, in preparing Friday's feast. And merci beaucoup."

Alfred Paul was the French Consul General in Richmond, had been for years before the secession and was the only French Consul who served throughout the four years of the war. He showed no pro-southern bias and was opposed to secession. His initial impression regarding the Union's naval blockade was that it would not be effective but time and event convinced him that the blockade was effective. Despite his lack of enthusiastic support of the Confederacy he was a great friend of Judah and Jules and one of their favored and frequent guests at Davenport House. They enjoyed speaking French with him; it was the only tongue spoken when the two were alone together; it was Jules' first language and it was Judah's second and favorite language. The Consul enjoyed the respite to return to the comfort of his native tongue rather than being forced to use the utterances of those gauche islanders on the west side of their misnamed channel.

Office of The Secretary of War, C.S.A.

After much anguish and thought, weighing the pros and cons of the various alternatives, the diabolical cerebration of Judah Benjamin came up with a scheme, wild and creative but daring and dangerous, potentially catastrophic in failure but supremely rewarding if successful. Yet, once again it is simple and the players are of the tested few. The objective, a successful recruiting meeting of McClellan and Hill.

Benjamin paused for a moment then continued his silent deliberation.

Hill was to use his retired U.S. Army uniform, cross into Union territory surreptitiously and proceed to Dr. Van Camp's dental office in Alexandria. McClellan would have received a letter from Hill urgently requesting a secret meeting with the particulars of the operation and the necessary precautions to follow. McClellan's trip to Van Camp's office for a sudden toothache with a 2 hours meeting for the approach, recruitment, acceptance (hopefully) of his acquiescence to meeting me must be planned and executed with perfection and without any delay. Time was of the essence. Hill was to be a missionary with the objective of convincing his beloved friend that a true salvation for an early end of hostilities and of peace in our land was at hand and that hand is yours Mac. God gave you that gift to use, not squander. At that point Hill was to identify me as the visitor who is looking forward with great anticipation to have the precious honor of meeting and bestowing upon him the title of savior of the land and culture we love. Hill will tell the general that convincing arguments will be made and detailed operational suggestions will be laid out.

Hill stops detailing my visit at that point in their discussions. I will elucidate and enumerate the few but vital instructions offered as suggestions so as not to embarrass or insult the easily affronted general. Such necessary things as mode and means of communication, daily detailed letters to lovely Madam McClellan of military and political matters, the use of equal parts of baking soda and water for secret writing in French only, when and if needed, code names, (his), "le clarion d'argent" (the silver bugle) and (mine), "Base," and follow up dentist appointment for the all important meeting with me. I will address these essentials at the appropriate time.

The Secretary sat back in his desk chair, stared at the ceiling and wondered out loud, he talked to himself a lot and liked hearing his own voice, "What am I missing? Oh yes, Hill must be briefed on my brainstorm and will see the logic and agree to it I hope. If not, I will formally order him to comply with the plan. He won't take lightly to the requirement to don his old uniform....that would make him a spy with a rope cravat if caught but that is unlikely, he is a bright and clever fellow. Also he must meet with Nelly before he meets with the general to get her acceptance, cooperation and briefing....that must be arranged and soon. I ordered him to make and execute those plans but haven't heard a word from him. I'll send a dispatch to him today by courier.

The Wallingford Cottage

"Ambrose, oh my lovely sweet Ambrose," Nelly Marcy McClellan crooned softly into his ear with her long blond locks unpinned falling freely about her face, her arms around his neck and his around her bare waist. " Oh how I long for you."

"You know you've always been my dearest and always will be Nel no matter what," murmured her Ambrose. She always called him that because he was either "Hill" or "Powell" to all others and "Ambrose" was her's alone. "We have but little time and every moment I am here we are both in mortal danger. My livery horse is saddled and ready to leave out back of the cottage; I must be on the road in an hour."

She squeezed his hands and asked in a worried tone, "Yes, I am greatly alarmed by your note. What matter is so secret and extremely critical to us, other than the war and," she pause and smiled, "and us?"

He pulled away from her, grabbed both of her hands in his, pulled her from the bed to her feet and gazed intently into her panicked, piercing sapphire-hued eyes.

He then swore her to secrecy, explained in detail Plan Target, its reasons of cause, its purpose, mechanics of operation, means of communication, manner of simple secret writing and emphasized her absolute invaluable role. She had few questions and was, as suspected, a quick learner. Best of all she was sympathetic to the efforts to bring an early peace and end to hostilities. She was agreeable to and receptive of her role with almost schoolgirl excitement. Hill was pleased and greatly relieved. The lecture was given, the lessons learned and the plan accepted in a shorter time than expected. This was a much appreciated gift of time, short that it was, for the mutual anticipation of the ecstasy of the consummation of their mutual love. Their crowning events were simultaneous and the post-coital shuddering prolonged. She clung to him as he left the bed. "Don't go, please don't go." she sighed. "But I must." His gaze fixed on her eyes and almost crooned the words," I love you." He proceeded to dress.

Before departing, Hill instructed Nelly to obtain a post office box in her new location and send it to his military address to continue their correspondence. Unhappily their next rendezvous was undetermined. Following a tearful expression of vows of mutual love, he left. Nelly fell to the bed sobbing, "Please God, keep him safe and let this not be our last earthly union."

Richmond, Virginia

In the evening's diminishing light, the "Dark Prince," as he was dubbed by his opposition, was walking back to Main street from the Gray House, overseen, rather overruled, by "Queen Varina" as dubbed by her detractors. I spend so much time there it has become like a second home. Poor Jules is so alone so often and for longer periods, he worries so. I must make amends somehow, be more attentive to his needs when together. Tonight, ah tonight will be ours.

He pondered the crises of the day as he strode down the street with a tempo metered by his walking stick taps, one for the right foot step with an occasional whip up to greet the passersby and a tip to the rim of his hat for the ladies. I must expunge my poor addled brain of the idiocy, tomfoolery and mendacity of the many absolute and intolerable fools with access to the President ---the ones with whom I must deal. They are uneducated, uncultured and gauche politicians and vendors who are put upon us as the plague---their only concern to enrich and preserve their personal domain.

"Enough!" he coughed aloud and thought, and now to the essentials that matter.

He had decided on a change of plans again. Hill would not be going to the dentist's office; too many details of travel that could go wrong, too much daytime exposure of Hill. He might be recognized having once been stationed in D.C., too much time in the enemy's uniform and if something went wrong the whole operation would collapse. So, instead and much better and smarter, he decided to kill two birds with one stone. He would have Nelly visit her husband in his headquarters in Alexandria, she residing in the Mansion House Hotel. The Southern sympathetic owner will be requested to make reservations for Abner P. Hollings of Bethlehem, Pennsylvania for the day Mrs. George McClellan orders a fine dinner for two at 1830 hours for room service in her suite. Mr. Hollings reservation will be for the room adjoining that of Nelly's suite. General McClellan's staff will make reservations for his wife some days before.

Hill disguised as a merchant from Bethlehem, Pennsylvania shopping for army contracts, with reservations for the suite adjoining Nelly's, will arrive in late evening and meet up with Nelly and the Bugle after their room service dinner. The warm reunion will be captivated by Hill's rehearsed presentation to his old roommate supported by Nelly. The plot, date, place and time of his sudden toothache would be established and confirmed. The identity of the Base who will meet the Bugle was to be revealed. Secrecy was to be paramount.

Benjamin was so excited about these changes, he gave the orders to the courier himself emphasizing the importance of immediate and direct delivery to the addressee, "even if it's in the middle of the night this dispatch must be given into the hand of the addressee."

He then gave orders to the network to alert James Green, the southern sympathizer and owner of the Mansion House Hotel, that Mrs. George McClellan, wife of the general, would be their guest for a few days. Security details would be explained by the guards on the day of her arrival. An in-room fine dinner will be ordered for her second day at the hotel.

Second. A room is to be reserved in the name of Abner P. Hollings adjoining Mrs. McClellan's suite on the second day of Mrs. McClellan's stay. Keep that room available for Mr. Hollings only.

Judah paused, leaned against a curbside hitching post, took a few deep breaths and congratulated himself for a most fruitful day of magnificent cerebral activity. Time to look forward to my respite with dearest Jules who is awaiting my arrival with great worried anticipation. Jules, wonderful and marvelous Jules, so innocent and loyal, so devoted, never questions my motives or actions, always accepting whatever I relate to him about my day's travails with a smile, soft and loving. What would I do without Jules? I could not survive without him...nor he sans moi.

He left the hitching post and started his short stepped pace again.

And now there are rumors about his not being among the conscripted for military service but specially privileged to serve as a clerk in the War Department. I put out counter rumors that the doctors considered him too frail to survive camp life. I must be his shield and buckler; in his own way he is mine.

When the key turned the latch and the door opened, there was Jules, all smiles and bursting with ebullience. Judah's world immediately turned French for Jules greeted him with a statement that he was awaiting this moment with great anticipation, in French, their household language. They embraced and kissed. Judah closed the door and they embraced again and kissed again. "I have missed you dearly." declared Jules. "And I you likewise but by two score more." responded his brother-in-law. And both knew they had developed into something more than brothers-in-law.

Headquarters of The Army of the Potomac, Alexandria, Virginia

Nelly had arrived by the morning train from Baltimore. It was the end of a long and arduous trip on multiple trains, with too many stops. She would wait for the general in his anteroom. She doffed her favorite travel weary Poke Bonnet, a few hand pats caused a cloud of tristate dust that generated a coughing spell. Exhausted, she flopped into the nearest chair and mused about her trip. All those stops in the middle of a wilderness. There were occasional stops at a settlement or town, at a rare city for water and coal and to take on and discharge farm products, freight and passengers. Even the best accommodations for the wife of the Commanding General of the nation's greatest army couldn't mitigate the journey's discomfort. The lurching and tossing about when standing, sitting or reclining was endless. The rhythmic racket of the train cars' squealing wheels against the iron tracks and the not so rhythmic rattle and squeak of strained cabinetry and furnishings of the passenger cars assaulted her ears. There was no quiet place. The upholstery and curtains emitted the odor of burnt coal and all exposed surfaces, table linens and uncovered food had a light sprinkling of smoke dust residue from the smoke stack of that culprit, the engine. The great iron horse is here, the modern commercial beast of burden and my husband is one of its engineers...personally I prefer the old fashioned flesh and blood horse. She left her chair went to the window, knew that her change of position would have no effect on bringing the general sooner but she was tired of sitting.

"May I offer you some tea Ma'am?" asked the orderly.

"That would be lovely," she replied, "Maybe that will take away the taste of the dust of the wilderness and the soot of the city," and giggled. She sat, pulled out her knitting bag and started working on a sweater that was new on the needles. Knitting allows her privacy, quiet time that she uses for critical analysis and problem solving. The sensory overload during the train trip failed to distract her from energizing her cerebral activity to formulate her plans to present a convincing argument for her husband's enthusiastic support and commitment to the success of Plan Target. Her knitting affords the opportunity to rehearse her plan of action. She knew that she'd accomplish her mission and win over the general with ease, after all she's been doing that routinely during their courtship and marriage.

As far as her husband's crossing the line, she knew that he already regarded the line between the blue and gray was faint, indistinct and absent occasionally. He need not look any farther than his cadet colleagues at the Point for justification and moral support. So many of them, and most of them his closest friends, had already made that decision and crossed that line. In fact he wrote to Ambrose that if he were in Ambrose's boots he would also have crossed the line.

Her knitting continued, an automatic mechanical, almost reflexive, activity; she could do it in her sleep. But both hemispheres of her brain were sending thoughts back and forth in rapid fire; she was fully awake and alert. So on she travelled on her stimulating mental journey.

The word treason should not be uttered during the discussion. That concept is associated always with separation, criminal intent and purposeful disruption or destruction of an extant political institution or government. Violence, too often, is an unwelcome accompaniment. Our cause is just, our methods humane and our mission is peace and prosperity for all our people and preservation of our culture and land. To accomplish our mission, in these times of war, already losing blood, property and treasure, it behooves us to make every effort to reduce those losses using the instruments and talents available. And we've got them... and you dear George are God's given conductor to produce this masterpiece of symphonic chorale. She looked up, smiled, pleased with herself and dropped into the bittersweet recall of their most recent encounter.

Ambrose, lovely Ambrose, when oh when? Please exercise the most caution in our endeavor. He was to arrive immediately after the fresh wine was delivered and the dinner cart was removed. I was to knock three times, pause and then two more and Hill was to appear through the door to the adjoining room. Then the frolic begins. The look on George's face will be memorable...I can't wait.

He was to arrive in late afternoon of the previous day under the name of Abner P. Hollings, a vendor from Bethlehem Pennsylvania, seeking government contracts. His room had been reserved days before by one of Ambrose's friends. He would leave the next day. According to his last letter, in response to my concerns about his being captured crossing the lines, he wrote that that was the least of his concerns and that I should fret not. But fret I do and will.

Her reverie was abruptly jarred into the present by a noisy return of the general with his entourage of staff officers and orderlies. The stomping of dust covered boots, jangle of their spurs, rattle of scabbards and the low mutter of the mob was suddenly interrupted by a familiar voice. Immediately a quiet fell over the room as a smiling McClellan, arms extended, marched across to Nelly announcing in a parade ground voice, "Gentlemen, I present my wife, the most perfect army wife on the rolls." He then kissed her extended hand and said softly? "Good day my dear, how was your journey?" Before getting an answer, he opened the door to his inner office and directed her to enter. "Please make yourself comfortable, I've got a few things to go over with my staff and I'll return. If you need or would like something use the bell on my desk and the orderly will respond."

"Oh but the orderly offered me tea a while ago and I haven't seen it yet," she remarked, "I'd like that please."

"Immediately my dear, I'll see to it." And he left.

Nelly sat on a straight backed, spindled armchair and took note of the office. It certainly didn't advertise all the comforts of home. The desk was a four-legged camp table covered in short stacks of paper and multiple maps, a double oil lamp graced the right upper corner. It was served by the general's chair and two wooden chairs, she was sitting in one, in front of the desk, all unupholstered. A four drawers filing cabinet stood behind the desk's right corner. Off to the side stood a wooden table larger than the desk with a few maps on it, most folded and a double oil lamp at the left far corner. No wood appeared polished. A coat stand stood on the left side of the front office door; there was a smaller door in the left rear corner, both of solid wood. The two windows were tall and had dark green faded drapes that were parted affording most daytime illumination. An empty fireplace was on the outside wall with a smoke stained wooden frame and mantle. and the hardwood floor markedly scuffed had no carpet.

A knock at the door signaled the arrival of her long awaited tea which she enjoyed along with a small delicious French pastry. Well, she thought, there is something good about this place.

It had already been established that she was not staying in the Headquarters, the Wilkes Mansion two blocks from the War Department, on Pennsylvania Avenue at 19th Street, on Jackson Square. The general was also happy about that. He had converted the first floor into his and staff offices and the telegraph office; the second floor was his personal apartment. She would have been unhappy with the lack of amenities, bare accommodations, unexciting menu and the cold and rigid routine of military headquarters. In fact she wasn't happy with the Mansfield House Hotel either, Alexandria's finest, but she remained there because it was the most convenient for the Target Project. It allowed easier and more frequent access to him to accomplish her mission and it was an essential part of the prearranged plan. For their critical sessions, privacy, safety and secrecy were paramount. What was to be discussed was too sensitive and vulnerable to detection if conducted in the headquarters' confines. Too many people needing to see the general, too many distractions, too many interruptions, too much interest in Nelly. Even at the Mansfield House, McClellan would place his bodyguards, not at the hotel suite's door but at the ends of the hallway and at the top of the steps to the floor. The rest of the bodyguards would be in the lobby, bar and around the outside of the building. No one was permitted on the floor where Nelly was staying without evidence of being a guest on that floor, one of the few authorized hotel staff, or a pass by the adjutant general or General McClellan himself.

On the night planned to execute her mission the general was to arrive at the Mansfield House at the appointed hour to dine and remain the full night. These were Nelly's absolute requirements, not to be cancelled or altered in any way. "And that's an order," she announced with gusto, in her usual manner of running their household. The general rarely if ever argued, balked or disobeyed. They both liked and accepted it; she wore the pants in the household.

VISIONS OF GREATNESS

On July 27, 30 and August 4, 1861, McClellan penned notes for a letter to Nelly indicating his whirlwind time in Washington and even on the way to D.C., arriving on July 26. He was enthralled by the enthusiastic receptions offered him by all whom he met from President to Cabinet, prince to pauper, citizens to politicians, private soldiers to senior officers and even from children at play. He delighted in it but, in a sense, thought it deserving, fitting and appropriate for one who was chosen by the hand of God to save the nation.

The second paragraph of that letter begins with. "I find myself in a new and strange position here---Presdt, Cabinet, Genl Scott & all deferring to me---by some strange operation of magic I seem to have become the power of the land. I almost think that were I to win some small success now I could become Dictator or anything else that might please me---but nothing of that kind would please me--- therefore I won't become Dictator. Admirable self denial!"

On August 8, 1861, during his Battle Royal with old General Scott for control of the whole Army of the United States of America, his first of many intense political skirmishes that would characterize his budding military career that eventually went afoul, he wrote to Nelly. "General Scott is the great obstacle---he will not comprehend the danger & is either a traitor or an incompetent. I have to fight my way against him & have thrown a bombshell that has created a perfect stampede in the Cabinet---tomorrow (August 10) the question will probably be decided by giving me absolute control independently of him................I receive letter after letter---have conversation after conversation calling on me to save the nation---alluding to the Presidency, Dictatorship &c............I feel that God has placed a great work in my hands---I have not sought it---I know how weak I am---but I know that I mean to do right & I believe that God will help me & give me the wisdom I do not possess. Pray for me, Darling, that I may be able to accomplish my task---the greatest, perhaps, that any poor weak mortal ever had to do. . . God grant that I may bring this war to an end & be permitted to spend the rest of my days quietly with you. . .I met the Prince (Napoleon) at Alexandria today & came up with him. He says that Beauregard's head is turned & that he acts like a fool. That Joe Johnson is quiet & sad, & that he spoke to him in very kind terms of me."

These early letters raise the distinct possibility that George Brinton McClellan's own head could get turned by the right turn of events by the right, or wrong, people---and there are some who are anxiously waiting and well prepared to do it.

Office of The Secretary of War, C.S.A., August 1861

Leaning back in his desk chair, arms folded across his pyriform abdomen, his puffy hands clasped with his forefingers steepled on his chin, the Secretary, alone in his office, was taking stock of the rapidly unfolding events of Plan Target. Let me see, I think things that had to be done are done and the actors have all played their parts perfectly so far and are readied for the coming events. McClellan remains in his headquarters in Alexandria, Nelly, apprised of, agreed to and sworn to the Plan is on her way to visit him and might already be there. She has already recruited Abigail Wallingford as her accomplice. Her residential requirements have been met as well as those for Hill as Abner Hollings. She has been prepared by Hill who is about to become Abner, meet up with Nelly and both of them will confront and prepare the general for my arrival. The dentist has been prepared. The French party is on schedule, the portly chef as Jean Paul St. Martin is officially assigned to ride in Consul Paul's carriage and he's chafing at the bit. The tailored coffin and the wagon are properly outfitted for the return trip and Joshua the freed slave driver is awaiting orders. Jules personally inspected and reluctantly approved the accommodations for my return trip. Did I forget anything? I don't think so and God knows I hope not. For Plan Target will launch in 2 days.

The obvious points of weakness are the line crossings of Hill and me, but mostly Hill's. I have others to aid and abet, he has but himself. But he is bright, resourceful, a soldier and knows the parts. He will do well. May the great Jehovah shed his blessings upon us all. And he reached for the decanter and snifter. On his second pull of brandy, he was struck by a new thought. What do I do with the intelligence I receive? I'm no general or field tactician; to be of value the intelligence obtained must be distributed to the appropriate battlefield commanders in a timely manner and in a form that fails to allow detection of its source.

Therefore, upon receipt of Nelly's correspondence from the Bugle and read by me the sent material will be copied by two clerks cleared, briefed and sworn in the matter, the material returned to me for return to Nelly through Jules and Abby. That way, if investigated, Nelly has in her custody and possession all letters sent her by her husband, guarded from vulgar gaze.

Despite all of this delicious adversity we have acquitted ourselves with exceeding audacity, creativity and perspicacity. Pray we are blessed with success. Ere we flagellate ourselves for failing to recognize the fact that we'd be better served had some of the sons of the Confederacy remained commissioned in the Army of the Union. Let us rejoice in the knowledge that our present Plan Target is all but secured. Its proposed effects are four fold those of the above alternative and will assure our rendezvous with destiny.

The Mansion House Hotel, Alexandria, Virginia

The dog days of August took their annual toll on all manner of man in Alexandria. The occasional hot breezes carried the Potomac River's moisture inland increasing the discomfort of the humidity. The sun-baked highways and byways gave off their contribution to the misery in manure-tainted dust. A sickening yellow mud in the sudden outburst of a summer thunderstorm offered its share. The natives were accustomed to their Augusts and despite their discomfort plowed into their separate fields of endeavor. With Nelly, it was a different matter. She was most distressed and suffered aloud and often, reminding all that she was only recently with baby. Alas, she checked into the Mansion House and inspected her suite, found it acceptable, not necessarily desirable but acceptable. She assured herself that a door to the adjoining suite existed and was functional by key from her side. She idled to the table bearing a complimentary bouquet of fresh flowers, sniffed a rose blossom, smiled and turned to the manager who accompanied her to the suite, "Lovely," she remarked, "thank you for such a kind welcome."

The manager smiled and gave a slight bow. "Please, anything the Madam desires will be our pleasure to provide."

Nelly moved into the sitting area. " Is there sufficient room here for a room service cart fully extended for a fine dinner for two tomorrow at 1830 hours?" using military time to impress the manager with her knowledge of things military.

"But of course Madam we will arrange things to your perfect satisfaction. Do you already know your desired menu, and if so I will ask you for it now. Otherwise, if you need more time for your decision of delectables please inform your butler, Jeremy, who has been assigned to your service." Spoken with the imperious tone of the major domo of the finest hotel in Virginia accompanied by a slight bow.

"Thank you sir, I will talk with Jeremy once we have settled in." Nelly turned to the maid who was unpacking her luggage to assist in the effort.

Thank God she didn't have May, her recent newborn first child with her, to feed and change and care for. She loved being a mother she told herself but it took work. Things would get better with time she was told. How do new mothers do it without the help that she has? Her nursemaid, Margaret, is a Godsend and so well endowed is she, May is always satiated when suckled by her. Oh well I have other things that concern me now. I hope Ambrose is unimpeded in his journey here, please God I need him. I can't wait!

At the other end of town, Ambrose Powell Hill was on the mind of another actor in this play. General George Brinton McClellan was in his headquarters about to ride off with his staff and his unusually large bodyguard of cavalry troopers to inspect a few sites for bedding down and training the huge number of new troop arrivals in the Washington area. Powell, his name for Hill, had written him a most interesting letter that was to be burned immediately after reading. He implored for a meeting as soon as possible and that he would come here and make all the arrangements for it; I was to await notification. Nothing have I heard of late. How he gets here not in irons or shot is his worry and not mine, thank God. But I know him and he is a sly old fox so I expect he will jump out at me at the most unexpected place and time in one piece and smiling, "hello Mac I miss you." And

McClellan broke out in a warm smile. I do wish we were brothers in arms instead of brothers at arms. Oh how I miss him, our mutual friends and the grand times we had on the Hudson. If only, yes, if only.

His orderly broke into his pleasant daydream with, "Ready, Sir?" And away they went.

His tour of Washington revealed few places to embed the massive number of new recruits, or areas to establish campsites to raise tents and build cooking fires. Troops were quartered in the halls of Congress, in churches, meeting halls and a veritable army of them were marauding the streets. Order was nonexistent, the city and environs were in chaos. Time for much needed organization and discipline and now. Once back at headquarters, he drew up plans and dictated orders to make attempts to remedy the crisis, knowing fully well that he would incur the wrath of the city fathers and his superiors at the War Department. His initiation into Washington politics at the highest levels was more like Baptism by fire, as he had already discovered to his displeasure and disquiet but he was no wallflower when it came to political intrigue and conflict. He had won the battle with General in chief, Winfield Scott, to be his replacement before Scott was ready to retire but he won with the enmity of quite a few of Scott's well-placed defenders. They all had long memories and desks in both houses of Congress or chairs in the Cabinet Room of the Whitehouse. They would be around for awhile. So be it. I too have a long memory, assailed for carrying grudges, and plan to exert my way with God's will.

He shuffled some papers, dictated a few memos and checked his schedule for the morrow. Oh yes, he remembered, fine dining with Nelly in her hotel suite at 1830 hours without delay. Punctuality has always been one of my strong points. But this evening, to show my dear army wife something of army life, she will dine with me and my staff of the fare du jour of the officers' mess at 1730 hours.

After another two hours at his desk, he retired to his upstairs sleeping room for a short kip after requesting his orderly to waken him at 1530 hours to prepare for the evening's festivities.

N/NE TO ALEXANDRIA

Hill was a nine miles ride west of Alexandria on the morning of the day appointed for his rendezvous with Nelly and Mac. He had planned his trip with good use of known and cooperative southern sympathizers, mostly slave owning farmers, army scouts and his own knowledge of the area from his days at the War Department with Davis. He had decided to take Champ, his great mount, with him to use for the last leg of his trip, a twelve miles ride on seldom used country roads from Fairfax station to Alexandria. He would also need Champ and his talents on the trip back. He spent a comfortable night after a sumptuous meal at the home of farmer Sheldon, a slave owner and father of two sons in the Virginia militia. He lived on the outskirts of Fairfax, Virginia, a few miles east from the train station. This shortened his ride to nine miles. Champ would appreciate that.

Hill had planned his journey using the Orange & Alexandria Rail Road from Warrenton Junction, Virginia, through Manassas Junction and Sangster's Station to Fairfax Station where he'd be domiciled at the Sheldon's spread. He'd then proceed on horseback to the Mansion House Hotel in Alexandria as Abner Hollings a Bethlehem Pennsylvania Moravian merchant in search of military contracts for his metal products. Prior reservations had been made for a suite that had been arranged "coincidentally" to be next to that of Mrs. McClellan by the hotel owner James Green, a southerner in heart and mind and surreptitious action.

This was if everything went as planned. In case of an unexpected event en-route, once he left Warrenton, he had the availability of emergent use of safe places by prior clandestine arrangements.

These were a Confederate widow's farmhouse near Manassas Junction, a livery stables near Sangster's Station owned by a trooper invalided at the Manassas battlefield and, of course, the Sheldon farm east of Fairfax. Furthermore, he had arranged to ride with his horse, Champ, in the car for mounts of passengers, other horses and mules for sale; cattle were privileged, they had their own car. That would serve a few purposes, avoidance of arousing the interest of the curious, garrulous, suspicious and the neighborhood gossip. He wasn't good at small talk anyway and he had much to think about without distraction.

Did he forget anything major or minor in his planning for this event? Was he ready to be a civilian in search of military contracts among the Union forces? Was his disguise adequate and did he know enough about his product to sound convincing if challenged by civilian or military authority. His exposure to any and all must be severely restricted. Thank God for the grand number of southerners who abide in the North, and how well organized they are....he smiled, Judah Benjamin is an amazing devil....truly a dangerous man. Remind me never to get on his bad side.

In his kit was a collection of drawings of items his foundry in Bethlehem manufactured for sale to the U.S. Army; horse bridles, axes, spades, picks and cast iron skillets. How's that for a load? Good I hope, he thought. But now to the most troubling problem at hand. He had documents attesting to who he was and what he did and why he was there. And his attire, including hat and boots and Champ's harness and saddle were fitting and appropriate and his weapons were two Derringers. He had second thoughts about his service revolver but wrapped it in his saddle blanket just in case. All was good once he was north of the lines in Union land. He was confident he could dissemble his way around anything that may crop up and he wasn't to be there long. He'll arrive in late afternoon or early evening, enter the Mansion House from the rear-loading dock area, pay an attendant to take care of Champ for the night, check in and carry his own kit to his suite and go from there. Then the real fun begins but he wasn't nearly as disquieted about that meeting with Mac and Nelly as he was about getting back across the lines the next day.

In his kit he had his old uniform and boots of a U.S. Army Captain and necessities of a C.S.A. field grade officer, emblems of rank and grey pants; the uniforms of the C.S.A. strangely enough, were not that much different from those of the Union forces because no regulation uniform was yet approved or available. In fact, some of the militia uniforms of the Southern states were copies of those of the Union troops. He had no document to guarantee safe passage across either the Union or Confederate lines. In fact the only documents of identity he had were the printed advertisements of his wares, with a Bethlehem, Pennsylvania address of the Hollings Tool Company and some bank notes of a private bank in Bethlehem.

Initially, he planned to use the reverse of his initial journey route as his return route but Benjamin put his thumbs down on that idea; he wanted Hill back in the C.S.A. as soon as feasible. So he ordered him to go south from Alexandria to Aquia Landing where the wharfs and rails were in well-protected Confederate hands. And Hill was to report to the Secretary of War without delay by rail from Aquia Landing to Richmond. Appropriate arrangements were in waiting for Hill's arrival in Aquia rail head. Champ was also welcome. Hill had a code name, "Heracles," given him by Benjamin that was known to the commanding officer of the military detachment at Aquia rail head of the Richmond-Fredericksburg and Potomac Rail Road. That officer was under direct orders of the Secretary of War to render every assistance to Heracles' efforts to get to Richmond without delay. Tentative dates for Heracles to arrive at Aquia Station were on or about August first.

Hill was riding through farm fields many of which were fallow following the disturbing consequences of the battle at Manassas

Junction. He was trying to avoid any Union patrols, most of which would be regulars and not the green volunteers. The Union forces were still licking their wounds and trying to get a functional armed force together with a lot of non-belonger youngsters running about in the overcrowded streets of Washington and surroundings. No self-respecting lad in Union blue was found too far outside the city limits of Washington, especially in the direction of that God forsaken, bloodied bit of real estate along Bull Run. And most of the blood that was shed there was blue.

Hill decided to follow a small fresh-looking stream into a wooded section to allow Champ a drink of bubbling shaded water and a rest under the canopy of the trees from the afternoon's heat. As he got farther into the woods, he could see up ahead a split rail fence that lined a road with a couple of stopped farm wagons. They were loaded with products for the shops and taverns of Alexandria which was about a mile up that road. The reason the wagons were not moving became obvious in a minute when two blue clad mounted troopers moved from the first wagon to the second. They halted at the driver's seat and engaged him in heated conversation. The farmer stood up in the wagon, didn't climb down, took off his hat and waved it toward Alexandria, his raised voice could be heard but his words were indistinguishable. He did not appear to be a happy man. The two troopers turned and went to the first wagon, made a gesture to the driver and the wagons began to move. The soldiers galloped off toward the town. A.P. patted Champ, cut an apple in half and fed the pieces to his happy mount. He walked Champ back through the woods to the open field, checked for unwelcome horsemen, mounted and set off for the Mansion House adventure.

THE WAR DEPARTMENT, C.S.A.

Judah Benjamin was irritable. He was alone in his office, finally. The day had been full of worried underpaid military officers and anxious overpaid civil servants scampering about the War Department all with problems but few to none with solutions. To clear the deck, he had to generate an artificial air of utter displeasure with all those about him. He had to finalize in his mind the most intricate details of Plan Target otherwise his recent acquired insomnia would continue unabated. So he rose from his desk chair to his feet with both arms reaching heavenward and belted, almost screeching, "Out! Get out---out I say, all of you! I am vexed; you have caused me rancor." He marched with vigor to the door opened it and with a sweeping motion of his free hand signaled for all to vacate and now. Recovered from the initial shock of the Secretary's abstruse outburst, the mortified mob competed to get through the open door so as not to be the last one in his Excellency's presence. And when the last one cleared the door jam the Secretary, with a vengeance, slammed the solid oak door that was felt the floor below. His stunned audience got the message---don't bother Judah Philip Benjamin anymore today.

Judah went to his desk chuckling to himself. You acquitted yourself with handsome perfidy and then he burst out laughing aloud. He opened the top drawer and removed a few blank sheets of writing paper, grabbed a one foot ruler and a pencil and went to a map laden conference table. He thumbed through a bunch, removed a few, cleared a space on the table, drew up a chair and sat down. Now I must once again study the construct, the timetable, and yes, the map. Time to put together again a logical and sensible order to quell my ravaged brain of this intracranial clutter of players, places, times, events. Yes and travel routes, emergency alternatives and vehicles. He paused, smiled and thought out loud, "yes, vehicles from the quadruped equine, the four-footed horse to the iron horse and from a buggy to a hearse with a farm wagon or two thrown in." This truly is an omnibus operation he thought as he enumerated the required, static accommodations, safe alternatives for two men and beasts and one freed slave.

He went to the huge safe standing not far from the fireplace. If files had to be incinerated in case of an emergency or to preserve secrecy, they were close to the flames. He opened the safe, removed an antique document box that was locked and unlabeled. He took it to the map table, pulled his pocket watch gold chain coursing across his pear-shaped abdomen. Delivered was his watch and a key attached to its ring. He opened the box and removed a couple of folders, all of which were labelled in French, and, in fact, all Target documents were in French. Even messages and notes from agents and operatives were translated and/or summarized in French---by lovely Jules St. Martin. The originals were incinerated. Just another brilliant espionage scheme dreamed up by Dearest Brother Judah, the diabolical genius. He opened the one labeled "Heracles" and thought, old Hill should be in Alexandria by now getting ready for the meet with the Target tonight, assuming all things have gone according to plan. Please God, let it be.

He got out the route map and studied it as he had more than once every day for the past week. The people and places were indelibly implanted in his mind. He too, like Hill, had no anxiety regarding Hill's journey to Alexandria. And there was optimism regarding the success of tonight's meeting with the Target and winning him over to meet with me. My major concern is, as is Hill's--- getting Heracles to Aquia Station and onto the Richmond Fredericksburg & Potomac R.R. Those first few miles of the forty miles from Alexandria south to Aquia Church would be the most threatening. Actually the real challenges will be crossing the lines between the two armies. Checkpoints and cavalry patrols must be anticipated, met and dealt with but once Pohick Church is reached, 11 miles by the Gravel Road and 17 by the Telegraph Road, there should be less risk of trouble. But getting there is the problem.

The document box was a stranger to his office in the War Department; its home was a large locked metal-strapped strongbox in Benjamin's study at the Davenport House. It had two keys, one carried in the beltline of Jules St. Martin's underdrawers and the other in a secret compartment hidden in the handle plate on the right side of the strongbox. It got a lot of use because the Davenport House study was the unofficial office of the Secretary of War. It was there that agents and special couriers, of which there were only three and not even St. Martin knew their real names, came and went at all hours of the days and nights. They carried scent of the dust from unrevealed places and the sweat of the persons with encrypted messages, parcels, federal greenbacks and even gold on occasion. This activity at the Davenport house would not generate the interest or suspicions that it would excite at the official offices of the War Department at the Mechanic's Institute. And Jules would be his aide, assistant, confidante and constant source of loving enthusiasm for his project.

Jules was privy to all that was going on; Benjamin tutored him in the artifices and machinations of the shadowed world of espionage. St. Martin was a quick learner and was morally and spiritually attuned. He was used as a loyal and secure sounding board, his closest associate, confidante, and lover, as some believed. He was actively engaged as a paid operative of the War Department. This also protected him from required active military service. He enjoyed the thrill of the clandestine and hero-worshipped agents Thomas Jordan and Thomas Conrad but he fell in love and shared his bed with young Benjamin Franklin Stringfellow. Dearest Judah took a dim view of that. He cooked for the secret visitors and was enthralled by their accounts of derring-do.

These comings and goings and late night visits, some hours long, were frequent and most unscheduled, or at least as far as Jules knew. Disjointed as they may have been, they eventuated in a working plan and network of spies and sympathizers, with equipment, mounts, buggies and wagons, routes and alternates and safe havens as needed.

Dearest Brother Judah instructed lovely Jules in report writing---intelligence report writing. Initially, he would translate all incoming dispatches and reports from only certain sources designated by Benjamin. With Jules' competence proven, Benjamin then requested only summaries to meet the increased number of documents to be handled.

If all went as planned, Jules would be working only on the correspondence of Target to Nelly and Base to Target. It would be absolutely critical to get the original Target-to-Nelly letters back to her as soon as possible so as to negate any Union counterintelligence investigation into the correspondence of Target to his wife. It would be common headquarters gossip and knowledge that their commanding general writes volumes to his wife almost daily. The content of those letters would be of much interest to some in high places in the Union as it definitely was to those in high places in the Confederacy. And those unfriendlies in Washington just might go looking for them; as Judah planned they would be there for the prying eyes to see.

The clock on the mantel struck three times, bringing Benjamin back to the matter at hand. Tempus fugit, he thought and put aside all other matters for now and thought of his own upcoming adventure into enemy territory to win the ultimate prize for the Confederacy, the control of the commanding general of the Union forces.

He would acquit himself successfully in obtaining a cordial, professional relationship... a mutually agreeable arrangement to assist in restoring peace, tranquility and sanity to our beleaguered nation. A concord that would reveal sound logic, unflawed reason and efforts to do God's will as a valid enterprise to any rational examiner. Thoughts of treason be damned and never to be pronounced. This is God's work for the betterment of mankind. We will be the shepherds of his flock....And I then returning triumphant....in the back of a hearse. At this thought he chuckled, moved across the room and reached for the brandy. He poured 3 fingers into a snifter, spun it a few times, and took a mouthful of the nectar, swirled it about, swallowed it and let out a loud and low sigh. "I'd give a purse of gold to be a mouse in Nelly's suite at this very moment."

The Mansion House, Alexandria

Nelly heard three short soft knocks on the conjoining door to the next suite. Her heart skipped a beat. She leapt from her chair, dropped her knitting and ran to the door, stopped, felt a little light-headed and spoke softly close to the door, her sweaty hand on the doorknob. "Yes, who's there?"

"Guess who." was Hill's response and he chuckled.

"I'll be there in a moment." she whispered and went to the maid's room, discharged her for two hours, requesting she place a do-not-disturb sign on the door on her way out and to so notify the sentries in the hallway. "The Madam would like an undisturbed short slumber before the night's dinner with her husband."

Nelly locked the suite door and rushed to the communicating door, opened it and fell into the anxious arms of her beloved Ambrose. The caress was intense with no spoken word initially. Finally its silence was broken by Nelly's almost inaudible, "Oh Ambrose, my Ambrose, I know what an eternity is. I have lived it since we were last together.

"I too my dear sweet." He responded as he carried Nelly to the waiting bed.

"Time is scarce," she murmured.

"And Sacred," he responded, as his lips and tongue explored her generous and heaving cleavage as his hands held her breasts softly while her erect rose-red nipples were being gently entertained between the tips of his fingers, soon followed by the moist warmth of his lips and his titillating tongue. She shuddered in ecstasy and moaned. She was panting, her heart was about to beat out of her chest as she unfastened her bodice and moved aside the impeding crinolines and petticoats. She had no time to completely undress.

He had become unshod and disrobed prior to his knocking on the door. Clad only in underdrawers, they were no challenge to her anxious hands that slid them down below his knees and then grasped his erect penis with one hand and caressed his testicles with the other. "Oh if only George could get so hard," she moaned and he kissed her extending his tongue onto hers and entered her below. They made love with a desperate intensity.

They couldn't enjoy the golden afterglow in each others arms sadly because of the upcoming critical meeting that could change the history of the world...or at least their world. They had a brief rehearsal for their roles in this one act play, hopefully not a tragedy but certainly not a comedy, and were confident in their ability to make it a success. George to her and Mac to him would be putty in their hands. They were both the sculptors who could render the piece a work of art...and they smiled in confidence. Nelly, a new person and madly in love, re-entered her own suite, freshened up and got redressed in elegant style for her imperious, barely-tolerable husband, the great general. Hill called for hot water and took a bath in the copper tub, one of four in the hotel. Ah, such luxury, he thought, might as well take advantage of it while I can. Then he dressed and ordered a light dinner in the suite. Dessert would be next door. Rather than the signal knock on the communicating door, he was to listen for the word "surprise" after their dinner and enter Nelly's suite.

General McClellan arrived as ordered, was greeted with the cool cordiality that was the accustomed and appropriate demeanor of the McClellan household, and moved to the sitting room.

Introductions had already been made between the general's staff and Nelly, so she welcomed them not as strangers. She was in an unusually good mood, sensed the general, for which he was very pleased. Drink orders were taken by the maid and hors-d'oeuvres were served. Conversation was driven by the general as expected and dealt with his accomplishments of the day and the week. Short of an hour, the general rose and stated that it was time for all his staff to leave at which point the staff thanked the hostess and took their leave. The general told his aide, who had just placed the general's valise on the floor next to the bootjack and placed his dress sword on top of the dresser in the bedroom, to come for him in the morning at 0800.

Once they were gone, Nelly asked her George if he was ready for dinner. Upon his affirmative reply she ordered the maid to ask for room service to bring the dinner, deserts and requested wines and then to leave; no server was required. And the maid was given the night off.

The food and beverages arrived, the table was set and the service staff and maid departed. Nelly informed the sentries in the hallway that she and the general were not to be disturbed unless Washington was invaded, the rebels were on the capitol steps, or General Beauregard was drinking a mint julip in the bar of the Mansion House Hotel...and she smiled and winked at the sergeant as she closed and locked the suite door.

Dinner proceeded with an air of formality; he was in his full dress uniform and she was adorned with yards of imported silks and exquisite lace. They engaged in small talk, mostly meaningless drivel, punctuated by two toasts by the general to, "your heavenly beauty," for the first and the "sublime tranquility you bring to our holy wedlock," for the second. Complimenting the occasion were the elegant Limoges bone china place settings, cut crystal glass goblets and stemware, languishing on a sculpted Irish linen table cloth with the napkins rolled in silver rings. The piece de resistance, undoubtably, was the superb fare of French cuisine with "absolutely divine sauces," in Nelly's words. The surprise was also a French pastry with a clotted cream sauce over fresh raspberries. The selected wines were French, and of the general's most favorite, and of course, the Brandy, the choice of Napoleon Bonaparte. Everything was French because the general was a Francophile extraordinaire and delighted in the fact that he was dubbed as the "little Napoleon" in the press.

Everything tonight was to please the general...and to prime him. Yes, he was to be happy, satiated and receptive to be honored with the opportunity of an audience with the great and storied foremost orator of the United States Senate, gloriously representing, formerly, the great state of Louisiana, Attorney General then Secretary of War of the Confederate States of America, the Honorable Judah Philip Benjamin. And this with an offer to be an apostle of peace...the apostle of peace of both the North and the South...the whole country.

"And now, my dear husband, it is time for your finest dessert," raising her voice, "a surprise, a surprise gift for you, a dessert beyond your wildest imagination." Nelly sang out with emotion as she turned to the connecting doorway through which stepped Ambrose Powell Hill.

The word "dessert" was the key for A.P. to open the door and greet his long lost friend, West Point roommate, fellow officer and co-worker under Secretary of War, Jefferson Davis and now opponent in war. Without a word spoken or a sword drawn, McClellan in shock, the two embraced like two old lovers. Genuine tears welled and fell on the cheeks of both. Still silent they drew back, but still holding the other at arms length, and looked into each other's eyes, each seeing the tears of the other. Words didn't come...couldn't come.

The moment was savored by Hill and McClellan...andNelly in her own way of mystified thoughts. Each man, a son of Mars, surprised at the strength of emotion, openly expressed and genuinely experienced. It was real. This instant of truth, a gift of God, set the stage for the coming play.

The cerebral commotion stirring within McClellan's brain and the quickened cardiac activity within his chest was a well appreciated surprise for Hill. Mac was moved; his gaze was intense but warm, the flush of his cheeks and the glare of the moist brow was congruous with his strong grip of Hills arms. The flash of memories of pleasure and pain, anger and laughter, failure and success, joy and sorrow, exhaustion and exhilaration were still active in the forebrains of both as Hill pulled away.

"Time to eat, drink and be merry, words come later." Nelly, breaking the electric silence announced as she directed, "you two boys to the table for some angelic French pastry and fruit and some nectar of the gods." They obeyed.

McClellan spoke first. " I got your letter. It is God's grant of my prayer to have you here fit and in full ownership of all your parts. I dare not inquire of your whereabouts and howabouts of your getting here in sound mind and body." And he laughed, " Only you Powell could do it.. A.P. Hill does the impossible once again. E pluribus unum."

Hill smiled. "Only for you Mac. I'm here for you as I've always been, from our days together in the long gray line till now and beyond. I'll always be there for you...I even gave you my best gaol." Nelly blushed, trying to hide it by bending low to pour the brandy into the waiting thirsty snifters.

"You struck a sensitive note in your letters," McClellan started, "especially the last. It is a subject of great concern to me personally and professionally and almost too much food for thought. I too wish we were wearing the same uniform."

Before Mac could finish his thought, Powell interrupted, one of his known characteristics, "We, you and I, are fighting for the same cause; we are marching under the same banner despite the color of our uniforms. We want to bring peace to our nation and restore our God given rights, for which our forebearers fought and died, the rights for life, liberty and the pursuit of happiness."

McClellan sat, silent and still. His gaze was fixed on infinity. Nelly fidgeted with her fingers and wished for her knitting. She reached across the table and gently placed her hands on the folded hands of her husband in a reassuring manner and sought soft eye contact with him.

This is going better than planned, thought A.P., Mac broached the subject. He broke the ice, the point that we thought would be the most difficult part of the play. Hill smiled and cast a furtive glance toward Nelly thinking, the best laid plans...and he quickly looked away. He stood with brandy in hand, stepped away from the table and apprised his old roommate from across the room. Now was the time for the coup de main.

"Mac," he said, drawn and deep, " What I am about to say to you is a mere echo of your own thoughts. I know you.... I know your brain... I know your heart..." He paused for effect between each statement. " I know your potential. You have the spirit and you know that God has gifted you for great acts and events, and yes you have the strength and spirit to meet those God given obligations to accomplish and fulfill his wishes. God showed you early that he had plans for you by giving you unusual talents in academic, physical and spiritual realms. You were fluent in French in your early teens, successfully completed two years of the University in Philadelphia, you were the youngest cadet at West Point, finished second in your class".... Hill paused, tilted his head and with a sideways glance laughed as he said," and had the best plebe roommate in the history of the Academy." McClellan shook his head in faked disbelief and laughed. Nelly looked surprised and gave a short forced giggle...Oh for my knitting she thought.

"I am a torn man, I must admit." spoke the target of the evening. "Despite the hue of our capes," he went on in measured cadence.

"We bleed the like crimson!" interrupted Hill, almost shouting.

The general nodded in agreement as he tightened his mouth, and retracted his lips against clenched teeth. " Both our boys bleed, no matter their compass point, staining the very earth that birthed them and destroying the nation that bred them. This is tragic. We must have peace."

Hill responded immediately, "That loud and uncouth set of Northern rabble-rousers spouting fire and smoke from their mouths like their mills and foundries belch from their furnaces and chimneys are determined to destroy our way of life. " Hill sounded like an evangelical preacher; the fire and brimstone was his. But his next outburst was delivered with a softer mantle of facial expression and gentler tone of voice.

"Mac, this war is a gift of God to you. This event introduces you to the world's stage." He paused, tilted his head and a smile played on his lips. The general shifted his rapt gaze from the blazing eyes of his dear friend to a point in near infinity. Nelly sat motionless in her chair, not making a sound, her eyes fixed on her husband. Her heart was racing and pounding with such intensity that her frontal lace was pulsing ever so slightly with each cardiac beat. She feared both of the boys could hear it.

McClellan left his chair, went to the floor-to-ceiling window, opened at the top to let the evening breezes offer some relief from the day's blistering heat and suffocating humidity. "The sun is setting over Alexandria," he said sotto voce. He paused, smiled, marched to the table, took his half full snifter, held it up in toast and in parade ground voice delivered, " Let us not live to see the sun set over our beloved nation."

"Hear Hear!" shouted A.P. as he grabbed his snifter and passed Nelly hers. "Hear hear," said she, emerging from her cocoon. They clinked their snifters and completed the toast. She sipped, the general a modest swallow but Hill a healthy belt.

"Now to the real reason you are here.....and, for that matter, the real reason I am here," McClellan remarked almost as an aside. He went into the bedroom, marched out of his formal footwear, slipped into his favorite carpet slippers and returned to one of the wing backed chairs. Hill took the other and Nelly was safe with her knitting and comfortable in the high-backed rocker.

Nelly, in a sudden burst of energy. dropped her knitting into its handbag, picked up her snifter raised it and said, with an element of drama, "To our fair nation, let it be so for eternity." She took a swallow before the two stunned men could respond. "The time is getting nigh, Powell must soon be on his way, treacherous that it may be, and you, my Dear General must get your beauty sleep to meet tomorrow's---the nation's demands and I must join you in bed to insure your sleep is beautiful. Now, you two boys, I know and love, have been tiptoeing around a truth we all know. So it is time to bring the bread out of the oven, slice it, butter it, devour it and call it a fine feast."

She turned directly to her husband. "As you have suspected, Powell and I have been corresponding for some time, in your behalf," accentuated by raising her tremulous voice slightly, dabbing her eye with her lace handkerchief for a feigned tear, "and more frequently since your most recent appointment. Yes, my dear, the gist of our communication has been you; your present problems, Scott and his backers for example, they are fierce and not a few. Then you have your near future with your historical vexation with superiors with whom you've already engendered their ire and they've engendered yours and finally the distant future of political power and high office....and as you've thought and expressed, residing in the White House as the Chief Executive, George Brinton McClellan, President of the United States of America. A nation once again united in peace and prosperity. This is reality George Dear. The nation needs you. In one of your most recent letters, here, I have it in my knitting bag." She pulled out a much folded, handwritten letter of three pages; McClellan recognized it as his own and a fleeting gentle smile crossed his lips beneath a decided frown.

"27 July, 1861," she read, "Aside from your literary adoration and oaths of perpetual love for me...which I cherish, brings a tear to my eye, a lump in my throat and a pang of heart, I was enthralled by your feelings and thoughts of yourself." She reached over, ran her fingers over the back of his and he produced a slight nod and smiled. She continued reading, 'I find myself in a new & strange position here---Presdt, Cabinet, Genl Scott & all deferring to me—by some strange operation of magic I seem to have become the power of the land. I almost think that were I to win some small success now I could become Dictator or anything else that might please me---but nothing of that kind would please me---therefore I won't become Dictator. Admirable self denial.' She stopped reading, looked at both men, held their gaze for a few seconds, smiled and announced, "I'm not finished, once I've got center stage, as you both know, I don't relinquish it with ease.

George, we all three here know and many others elsewhere, former West Pointers, business and civic leaders know that you are the one man who can lead this nation and the campaign train starts here."

A.P. jumped to his feet. He had to have his say and add his two cents.

"Mac!" he cried, "A great man, a brilliant man, a powerful man, a gifted visionary wants to meet with you. He and you are so alike in many ways. You both, together, have the potential to assure our nation's survival.

And he, with great risk, will come to you to enlist your genius in engineering a survival plan for our nation....and he plans to conduct the meeting in French." Hill pulled back, tilted his head and gave a slight twisted smile that McClellan knew well from former close encounters with his old roommate. "He knows you Mac, he has studied you."

"And who is this grand resident of Olympus who speaks French?" Mac questioned, reaching for his brandy, eyes glued to Hill's.

Hill pulled himself to full parade ground bearing, looking straight into the general's eyes and said. "General Sir, a confidential audience with his Excellency, the Commanding General of the Union Forces, is requested by the Secretary of War, formerly the Attorney General of the Confederate States of America, his Excellency, Judah Philip Benjamin."

S/SW TO RICHMOND

Having left the general and his lady in good spirits and stead, he made his way from his suite where he donned his Union blue britches and blouse, booted, gloved, he had secreted his saber in Champ's saddle blankets at the start of his journey in Virginia.... it seemed like years ago.

Hill had left his packed knapsack just before dinner, with a bonus for the porters on the loading dock at the rear of the hotel whom he had paid on his arrival to be Champ's minders. They liked that "Pennsy Dutchman, he's free wi de coins."

To avoid the hallway sentries he went onto the balcony of the suite; the street below was quiet, empty and dark. Perfect. He slid over the wrought iron railing, like the athlete he was, onto a ledge on the floor below. Hugging the wall and using whatever hand-holds were available, he inched along to the first window which was darkened and closed but not locked. A Godsend. He lifted the sash without a noise, stopped, listened while his eyes adjusted to the darkened room. The only light was an orange slit under the door to the hotel corridor. The room appeared to be unoccupied. Thank God, so far so good. He moved to the hallway door, put his ear to it, listened and heard nothing. He unlatched the door and opened it a crack, still no sound so he opened it far enough to see to the end of the corridor, still no sound or body. The same for the other end of the hallway which housed the service stairway. So, out he went and down the service stairs to the loading dock.

The two porters were asleep on piles of straw with an uncorked bottle standing guard next to one. Neither stirred. And there was Champ, getting to his feet from a recumbent position on his own bed of straw. A half bucket of oats and a nearly full bucket of water stood near by and Champ approached them, as if he knew there was going to be an upcoming adventure. Hill smiled. "Good boy, good old Champ, do you know something that I don't?" he said as he patted Champ's neck. The horse nodded his head twice and whickered in the pleasure and knowledge that he is in the presence of his master.

Hill grabbed his knapsack, from the shelf in the stall, retrieved his holstered sidearm, unwrapped his saber from the saddle blankets, strapped it on and adjusted the peak of his kepi. He chuckled to himself thinking, this is the only part of my old uniform that still fits and goes on without a struggle. I must remember to tell some of my colleagues who think my hat size has increased since my recent appointments. He walked Champ to the street, mounted him and walked him into the darkness...of the night...the darkness of the nation's future...of his future...of Nelly's future...of Mac's future...but right now, this instant I must concern myself with the potential for real and immediate dark episodes.

A small party of staggering troops singing bawdy songs loudly and laughing was leaving a tavern down the block and weaving toward him. He moved Champ to a canter directing him to the left side of the street as he approached the party, hoping their disturbance of the peace would not bring out the Provost Marshal's curfew monitors.

He slowed Champ to a walk when the party started to spread across the street blocking it and directed Champ to the center of the street. The crowd fell silent and stood staggering in place looking at the Union Officer on horseback.

"Out late aint ya sir?" rasped one reveler, then laughed and coughed. As Hill rose to a stand in his stirrups, holding the reins in his left hand, raising his right gloved hand with his palm down, he was about to speak when the soldier at the right end of the waving line coughed and vomited. A few of the men laughed. A heavyset man in the center of the line, where Champ was pointed, staggered forward and grabbed at Champ's bridle. Champ reared and standing on his hind legs flailed both front legs striking the assailant on his right shoulder. There was a scream, the bleeding man went down and his fellows dispersed. Champ galloped off to the reassuring neck pats and words of his master.

Hill had decided to risk wearing his U.S. Army uniform wearing the rank of Captain, in getting through Alexandria, by the use of back alleys, private estate lanes and footpaths that Champ could navigate blindfolded as long as his master was in the saddle giving directions by gentle tugs on the reins, knee pressures on his ribs and soft spoken verbal commands in his left ear. Champ was also whistle and hand signal trained. There were reasons he was named Champ.

A.P. thought he'd fare better in his departure from Alexandria by leaving the Mansion House in silence in the half hour after midnight. Curfews meant little to the hard-boiled regulars and the new recruits were quick learners. Most of those milling about in the streets or staggering in the alleys of the after-hours and off-limits ale houses were out of uniform in the stifling heat and humidity and could give a tinker's dam about some mounted Union officer passing by. Mac was still struggling with the undisciplined numbers of troops who were arriving into Washington and Alexandria. The Provost Marshal's Office was severely undermanned and untrained. So he wasn't troubled about Alexandria but the roads leading south were the worry. He debated in the solitude of his own brain before arriving in Alexandria, which road south would be the most accommodating to provide his safe and unimpeded escape to the safety of Aquia Church.

Telegraph Road, Accotink Turnpike, the Gravel Road and Little River Turnpike were the main and known roads that were available. Of those, according to his most recent intelligence reports, Accotink Turnpike was the less patrolled road. Fort Willard was its main provider of road patrols and sector security and Fort Willard, in name only, was a makeshift artillery park of a half-baked battery. That route would not be the shortest in distance or time but, he thought, less hazardous and he planned to skirt the main road by riding a safe distance in the fields parallel to it where possible. The potential trouble spots will be where the road penetrates heavy wooded or scrub areas and crosses bridges. But Champ and I will do it.

He had also considered one of two alternatives for navigating Confederate territory once out of Blue country where his Union Army officer's uniform would grant him some element of safety if challenged. His northern cover story would be based on his duty with the Coastal Survey Division of the War Department. His ostensible mission was to collate findings for coastal and heavy artillery placements along the Potomac under the cover of darkness so as to avoid alerting the curious rebels. But on the south side of the line he'd adopt a new persona but remain in his Union officer's uniform. If and when he was challenged or arrested, mostly when, hoping he would be arrested or challenged before he was shot, he would offer the following legend. He would be a native Virginian who had been a serving officer in the United States Army, now having resigned his commission from the U.S. Army, he was heading home to fight for his home state of Virginia. If that failed to gain his passage and he was detained or about to be hanged or shot, he'd immediately demand to be taken to the arresting party's commanding officer. That's assuming the party who captured him were not hooligans who called themselves irregulars. Once in the presence of a legitimate regular officer of rank and some authority, Hill would state that he was operating as an agent of the Secretary of War of the C.S.A. and that an immediate telegraph message should be sent to him in Richmond stating that Heracles' mission impeded by his incarceration at such and such Headquarters by so and so officer of the Virginia Militia. Immediate reply required.

signed, Heracles.

With wishful thinking he hoped he wouldn't need to invoke that option.

He was nearing the outskirts of Alexandria, on a slow walk for Champ; who knows what might be in store for him down the road. So to clear his mind of the potential complications awaiting ahead of him, he thought back to last night's grand affair. It went better than he expected. It was Nelly who cut to the core. When she dropped her knitting, picked up her brandy and took a gulp, I could see that old expression that I knew so well, she means business and now. And he broke the silence of the darkness with a loud laugh. Champ whickered at the sound of it.

Time to take to byways rather than the highway, he thought and reined Champ into a roadside field of young corn and headed south keeping about 50 yards from the turnpike keeping Champ at a fast walk, keeping an eye out for army patrols.

He resumed his prior line of thinking... I really think that Mac had a sense of what was coming, what with my letters and the slow press Nelly was exerting on him. He had already analyzed things that he knew about those with whom he was dealing now and would be dealing in the future and he knew about himself, his strengths, weaknesses and desires. He was no fool. But the appeal to his ego and ambition was the key to our success. I was a tad surprised when Mac agreed to grant an audience to Benjamin without a lot of persuasive points of argument. I was proud of my use of the "granting an audience" device in my persuasive argument---I knew that would get his attention and he'd like it.

I'm sure after I left that Nelly carried on with our plan to assure Mac that his decision to grant an audience to Benjamin was not only appropriate and just but was the only logical decision that a sane man could conclude. She would also replay the script for the scenario of Mac's toothache and dentist visit. Now I've got to get to Benjamin as soon as possible to assure the success of our sacred mission. As that thought crossed his mind, Champ nodded his head twice and whickered. Hill's attention had an abrupt awareness of a passing cavalry patrol on the turnpike opposite to his direction. The darkness and distance negated a visual confirmation but the sounds indicated a number of riders proceeding at a trot heading toward Alexandria. He halted Champ and had him lie down. They were in a field of wheat, too early for any cover. When the sounds of the patrol were almost inaudible he got Champ back on his feet and made for the turnpike. He graduated from trot to full gallop; both he and Champ were ready for a fast pace. He reckoned he was not far from Pohick Church where he planned on taking a short break for Champ's apple.

The Davenport House

Undisturbed slumber was a rarity nowadays, thought the Secretary of War as he rolled about in his oversized 4-poster bed. Jules was down in the kitchen making breakfast that he'll bring up when I tug on the pull sash. Poor dear Jules, he is fretting about my upcoming trip into enemy territory. Actually, I am looking forward to it with great anticipation---a new adventure and a welcome change from the hum drum of reading daily reports from the field, roll calls, endless requests for men, beasts of burden and beasts to eat, arms, ammunition, uniforms and lest I forget, shoes. Will this war ever end, my heart requests, it just started responds my brain. So he rolled out of bed and slid into his slippers and reached for his silk robe, tugged on the bell sash and sat at his small table brushing the documents to the floor. "Blasted papers, they are all over my life, both waking and sleeping," his voice breaking the silence of his bed chamber. "I have nightmares of hurricane winds roaring through my chamber's windows ripping telegrams, letters, reports, papers and more papers, all secret, from my desk and tables blown into the darkness of the vast beyond. And they all need my comment and signature but they are all gone. I waken in a torrent of chilling sweat and a racing heart. I must tell myself that it was but a dream, thanks be to the great Jehovah." He wiped his sweating brow with the laced sleeve of his robe.

There were three soft knuckle knocks to his bedroom door and Jules appeared, pushing the door open with his foot, holding a tray with a breakfast for two.

"Bon jour mon cher Judah," were the first words Judah Benjamin heard that morning other than his own.

“Bon jour mon amour,” Benjamin responded. They both smiled as Jules placed the tray on the table and pulled up another chair.

The conversation, always in French when they were together except when commanded by Benjamin, “English only,” covered the night’s slumber, plans for the day for each, household problems, the conduct of the war and, most important of all, coming events, especially that one coming event that causes Jules nightmares.

“I am really anxious about my trip north but pleasantly anxious,” Judah stated as he extended his hand to cover that of Jules. “You must not fret, my love, I will be fine and will enjoy the event, coming and going. rather going and coming.” He chuckled and dabbed a drop of apple butter from his chin with his napkin. “ I will be returning to your lovely waiting arms earning for our embrace and our lovely time together.”

Jules feigned joyful acceptance of Judah’s attempts to put his fears at bay but Judah saw through his thin disguise, left his chair went to Jules and took his head between his hands, looked into his eyes, kissed both closed, tear moistened lids and then kissed his lips. He held his head for an extended moment, staring at Jules’ closed lids. Jules opened his eyes, tears welling, he stood up and embraced his lover. Hand in hand they went to the bed.

South Of Pohick Church, in "Reb" Country

Having rested at Pohick Church after an uneventful ride, both rider and mount were refurbished, Champ with a ten minute rest, some water and an apple, and A.P. with a cigar and 3 fingers of brandy. They were galloping when using the turnpike and fast walking in the fields of clover, wheat and young corn. Daylight would soon be breaking and the next rest stop was to be Woodbridge, an eight miles ride from Pohick. Farmer's wagons would be expected soon and the horse soldiers' patrols would be expected once daylight was established. His plan was to avoid those patrols if possible. But he wasn't sure whether to skirt Woodbridge by farm lanes, roads and fields or to enter the town itself. Six of one and half a dozen of another, he thought.

He came upon a farm wagon coming out of a lane that turned onto the turnpike heading his way. He had passed some structures, some farm houses, barns and out buildings along the way but no visible light in the windows of any making him feel very alone but this farmer and his wagon was a welcome sight and he doffed his hat as he passed him.

Before he knew it, he was on the outskirts of Woodbridge. Oh hell, I'll just ride into town, he thought, and put Champ into a fast walk, perusing the objects in his peripheral vision. Best to find the livery stable or the blacksmith...no better place to find out who or what is coming or going. He heard the tell-tale clang of the hammer on the anvil and turned down an alley toward the source of the noise. He was in luck because the livery stable was attached to the blacksmith's shop. He reined in Champ, dismounted and offered a pleasant greeting to a bearded brute of a man in a long leather apron who raised his hammer bearing, sweat-soaked arm in response. "what brings ya har, " he grunted.

Hill stated that he was on his way to Richmond to join the Confederate army. He asked if his horse could be checked for a broken shoe and could he buy a bucket of oats. The blacksmith came from behind the anvil, spat a chaw of tobacco, looked Hill in the eye and said he'd look at the hooves and shoes and sell Hill a bucket of oats. Then Hill pulled a blanket from his kit and asked where he might lie down on a couple of hay bales while Champ got shod and fed since he'd been on the road dodging Union patrols all night.

"No blue coats round har unless em dead, prisnehs or runaways," replied Caleb Smith with half a grin, "hep yuself." He had a distinct limp but his bare uppers were well muscled. He grabbed Champ's reins and led him to an empty stall. Hill followed, threw his blanket onto some clumps of straw and climbed aboard. He was snoring in minutes.

When Caleb got back to his anvil, he had guests. James, "Little Jimmy" Martin, Lem Jones and Tommy Longturn, three hang-abouts who were in need of a bit of the dog that bit them the night before in Sullivan's saloon. Tommy was their boss and the only one of them who could read. "Caleb," he started, as he leaned from his saddle, "We saw a yank officer come your way a while ago. Where'd he go?"

Caleb gave his half grin and nodded toward the stall where Hill was sawing wood with a vengeance. "He's on his way down Richmond to change sides or says he."

"He's a damn yank and worth money Caleb...a bounty if we turn him in." the leader snarled. He dismounted, and so did his cohorts. "Caleb, you look the other way an me an the boys will rid you of this pest but only after we empty his pockets and give you a share to cover your cost and then some. We'll just bind im up, blindfold im, throw im across his horse and head for an army bunch that'll take him off our hands an pay us a bounty. We'll cut you in." Tommy smiled, "Don't that sound good boys?" And Little Jimmy and Lem nodded and grinned.

"Ah don't see nothin, the horse is well-shod and fed and watered---the yank owes me two dollars fifty, my copper bucket is on the stove. Go out the back an be quick." Caleb gave his half smile and limped off to his office and shut the door.

Tommy gave orders to his co-conspirators; Little Jimmy would bind the feet; Lem, since he was all muscle, no fat and no brains, would strong-arm the arms and forearms behind Hill's back, bind the wrists. and bear hug Hill to his feet, holding him while Tommy put a feed bag over Hill's head. They'd then throw Hill over Champ's saddle, with his head tied to the left stirrup by a rope around his neck and his ankles tied to the right stirrup. Hill would be attacked simultaneously by Little Jimmy and Lem while Tommy pressed the muzzle of his pistol hard against Hill's temple shouting at Hill that his head would be blown off if he resisted. This was the plan and they set about pulling it off.

Hill was in the midst of a REM state dream that evolved suddenly and violently into a waking nightmare. A heavy weight was upon his legs and pain about his ankles while his torso was twisted and his arms were pulled behind his back causing pain in his shoulders and wrists. At the same time he felt a painful pressure in his right temple as someone pulled his hair and shouted in his ear something about blowing your brains out. He struggled but nothing responded and shouted as something was pulled over his head that smelled like stale oats. Then he felt a sharp pain in his head and the last thing he remembers was the smell of stale oats and seeing a silver-blue lightning bolt in his dream. Tommy thought the yank was not a cooperative captive and he was strong and wiry so he struck Hill's head with the but of his pistol. Hill's limp body was then thrown over the saddle of Champ and secured to the stirrups.

The three highwaymen left Caleb's stables out the back way with Tommy in the lead with the reins of Champ, who was second followed by Little Jimmy and Lem bringing up the rear. They headed south on the road to Dumfries talking and laughing about the bounty they'd get for the yank officer added to the $50.00 in gold, $120.00 in greenbacks and the gold watch and wedding ring they looted from Hill. "Sure's a fine horseflesh he's got." stammered Little Jimmy. "Well we'll see bout that when we turn im in." responded Tommy. Lem. dumb and happy, taking swigs from his water bag which was really a fire water bag. Hill, in the meantime, was slowly recovering from the blow to the head and the smell of stale oats had been replaced by that of fresh vomit. His head was throbbing and every muscle in his body was on fire. The feed bag had a fairly large hole in its bottom so that he could see the stirrup and side of the horse to which he was tied and to his surprise and delight he recognized the stirrup as his and the horse as Champ. Well all is not lost he thought but he heard bits and pieces of the boys talking about a bounty for a yank officer....that may not be good. Only time would tell. And he fell into another mental cloud of half consciousness. These in and out phases occurred a couple of times and each "in" time was getting longer and clearer but the discomfort worsened. Yet he remained silent. Finally he had constant wakefulness and clarity of thought.

The day was hotter and therefore he felt it was late morning or early afternoon when he heard a shout and his horse came to a halt. There was conversation between one of his party, the smarter sounding one of the bunch with a distant voice, heard but not understood. Then the distant voice came closer and had a distinct quality that Hill recognized immediately and he rejoiced, It was the voice of a military man. With all his might and available loudness he could generate from his weakened general state and from within his hood he shouted, "Soldier hear me out. Soldier, hear me out now." And there followed an immediate silence of all parties for a few seconds that seemed like an eternity to Hill. Then a command was given and Hill saw a hand untying his head from the stirrup and he was lifted to his feet, unhooded, and untied. He smiled and saluted the soldier in charge of the cavalry patrol which had halted his captors and said, "Take me to your commanding officer immediately. This is urgent." Hill rubbed his elbows and wrists, twisted at the waist to both sides, flexed and extended as if readying for a run. The Cavalry officer looked perplexed. Hill couldn't tell his rank; whether he was a non-commissioned or commissioned officer was not apparent by his uniform or lack of it but he thought it better to treat the trooper as if he were junior to him in rank but with respect. Then his captor-host-savior barked an order to his patrol and his prior trio of captors dismounted and were searched by the troopers.

"You'll find my pocket watch and wedding ring in their loot and about $50.0 in gold and a little over $100.00 in paper I had in my pockets," Hill said as an aside. " But now I must demand as one soldier to another that I be taken to your commanding officer as soon as possible."

"I sir, am Sergeant Jason Randolph of the 4th Virginia Cavalry. You are in my custody and will be treated as a prisoner of war with all the courtesies and restrictions that apply. I will take you to my headquarters where your disposition will be determined. So if you will, sir, mount up and we'll get started. Hill gave a warm smile, saluted and said, "Thank you and carry on Sergeant."

Tommy, Little Jimmy and Lem were huddled together, standing in the shadows of three mounted troopers, watching this scene when Tommy shouted, "Where's our bounty?" He received no reply. As Sergeant Randolph and Hill walked their horses by the terrible trio, Champ stopped, approached the three, nipped Tommy's shoulder and he screamed. Little Jimmy and Lem started to move away when Champ lowered his head and grabbed Little Jimmy in the right buttock and stepped on Lem's foot with his right hoof. They both yelped. Hill reined in Champ, patted his neck, leaned over and said softly, "You're alright Champ." Champ nodded, neighed and got up with the Sergeant's horse. "That one's gonna have a rough time sitting in a saddle for awhile," observed the sergeant and he laughed. "We're heading to Dumfries so we'd best be getting on and they went to a gallop.

THE MANSION HOUSE

Back in Alexandria, Nelly was overly attentive to the desires and needs of her general since the dinner with her true love Powell. McClellan sensed it but accepted and enjoyed it. And it gave him more comfort in his decision, as he pondered, which was, after all, God's wish for him to meet fully his noblesse oblige. A gnawing concern of my soul has been allayed, a great weight has been lifted from my shoulders, thus the resulting comfort of acceding to the desires of the Great Jehovah. Thy will be done! And he smiled to himself in a quiet sense of joy. I can't wait to meet the great Judah Benjamin. I can't wait to make great things happen.

Judah Benjamin, in the meantime, was most uncomfortable in anticipation of the news from A. P. Hill. Where is he...his silence is deafening and the anxiety is overwhelming. Bad humors have sapped my soul. He rendered a soft moan that didn't go un-noticed by Jules across the room. "My dear Judah, is there something I can do to assuage your turmoil?" he offered.

"No No dear one, fret thee not, I must suffer my mental tortures in solitude. But your concern warms the cockles of my heart," he smiled, rose, walked to the window and stared at the clouded sky.

A Slow Road to Richmond

The ride to Dumfries went undisturbed and seemed shorter than anticipated; there was little conversation between the Sergeant and Hill. The smell of freedom was perfumed by the roadside honeysuckle and Hill took a couple of deep breaths and started whistling Dixie and the sergeant smiled and nodded his head. The road started to get busy with empty wagons coming out of town and loaded ones heading toward it. A cavalry patrol approached and the sergeant brought a halt to his party. The Sergeant saluted the officer in charge of the newcomers, exchanged a few words, pointed toward Hill who saluted the officer and nudged Champ to approach him. "Good day sir," Hill addressed the officer who nodded and touched the brim of his cap.

"My sergeant tells me that you demanded to be taken to his commanding officer, well sir, I am he, Lieutenant Robert Harrison!" Hill smiled and replied, "Sir, I place myself in your custody and expect the courtesy to be taken under guard to your regimental headquarters without delay.

The Lieutenant bristled, "I remind you sir, you are in no position to demand or give orders but you can rest assured that you will be escorted to our headquarters in Dumfries post haste. I'm quite sure our Colonel would like nothing more than the pleasure of your company, he said with a sarcastic smirk. He turned in his saddle, ordered two of his troopers to ride aside Hill in the middle of his column and started down the road to town at a gallop. Hill smiled and Champ enjoyed the change from all that standing on the road to galloping on it.

THE DAVENPORT HOUSE

Judah Benjamin was almost in spastic delirium. He had insomnia, anorexia, nausea, intermittent abdominal cramping and diarrhea, occasional cold sweats and his brandy imbibing had markedly increased. Dear Jules was beside himself in worry.

"I've got so many loose ends that I don't know which ones to tie together," he blurted out one evening at the dinner table with an untouched plate of food in front of him as he gulped at least two fingers of brandy. I must hear from Hill, that McClellan is not just anxious to meet with me but is agreeable to our proposal and if not agreeable, at least not hostile to it. The date of his tooth ache, the dentist's appointment, the Royal French entourage, my arrival, our discussion in the dental operatory, my departure in the hearse, my transfer to a carriage to Aquia Station and from there, by rail, home to your anxious arms and stricken heart. A courier will alert Madam Nelly, the dentist and the undertaker for the hearse as to the date the operation begins. Our people this side of the line will be made ready for my funereal arrival. All orders and messages are verbal, not a word is written. He chuckled and Jules rejoiced in that slight show of comedic emotion, the first time in a long time. "Oh Hill, where for art thou, come soon." He lifted his half-filled snifter, rose from the table and left the room. Jules remained, pained in place.

Dumfries, Virginia

The Major, Randal Starling, well-appointed in his nutmeg blouse and cavalry boots over sky blue trousers, presented an impression of professional competence sitting behind a folding camp desk on a canvas backed folding chair with an undisguised air of skepticism. In his Colonel's absence, he was in command and was enjoying it until this upstart yank officer arrived on the scene with a strange story and stranger demands.

"Major, my compliments" Hill stated with authority, "this matter is of the utmost importance and urgency. I assure you sir, that any misgivings you have will, be allayed by the return telegram from His Excellency, Judah P. Benjamin, Secretary of War. I am under his orders on a mission that must remain 'devoid of vulgar gaze,' in the very words of the Secretary. You must send the following message and without delay." Hill requested and received pen and paper. He scribbled a few sentences, turned to his captor and asked his name, rank and headquarters address there in Dumfries for return purposes. He finished his message and signed it "HERACLES."

"Major, this message must be sent immediately and you will receive a reply post haste. I thank you sir. And now sir, I am at your service."

THE WAR DEPARTMENT, C.S.A.

Three knocks on the heavy oak door and it opened with an excited orderly holding a document that was a telegram marked. "Urgent, Immediate delivery to addressee only, make no copy." It was addressed to "His Excellency, Judah P. Benjamin, Secretary of War, Confederate States of America." Judah, grabbed it, read it and jumped to his feet shouting, "Eureka, God is great, God is good! The great Jehovah has spoken. And we his humble servants will respond accordingly and immediately. His orderly was both shocked and pleased at his Secretary's response. His shock was he had never seen such a demonstration. His pleasure was that the Secretary's mood had been dark and sour for weeks but now there was a welcome relief.

Benjamin sat back down at his desk and started writing his response to the telegram from Dumfries. It consisted of four sentences,

> TO : MAJOR RANDAL STARLING, OFFICER COMMANDING, DUMFRIES VIRGINIA ARMY POST
>
> FROM: JUDAH P. BENJAMIN, SECRETARY OF WAR, CONFEDERATE STATES OF AMERICA
>
> EXECUTE ANY & EVERY ASSISTANCE TO FACILTATE HERACLES' ARRIVAL AT THIS OFFICE IMMEDIATELY.
>
> THIS OPERATION AND ANY KNOWLEDGE OF IT IS MOST SECRET AND DIDN'T OCCUR. YOU ARE ORDERED TO SIGN AND DATE THIS DOCUMENT

OF AFFIRMATION OF YOUR OATH TO ACCEPT THE REQUIREMENTS OF THIS DOCUMENT. FURTHER YOU ARE ORDERED NOT TO HAVE THIS DOCUMENT COPIED AND TO DELIVER IT DIRECTLY AND IMMEDIATELY AFTER READING AND SIGNING TO HERACLES.

IMMEDIATE RESPONSE REQUIRED.

Benjamin handed the note to his orderly, "Send this immediately and stand by the telegrapher until it is sent... and if an immediate response is not received have my message sent again with a subscript of, "AWAITING IMMEDIATE REPLY OR FACE COURT MARTIAL FOR FAILING TO OBEY ORDERS. BY ORDER OF SECRETARY BENJAMIN."

Although the Secretary was beaming and overjoyed, his orderly knew he meant business and wasted no time in getting to the telegraph office. Benjamin did a little gavotte and hummed to himself as he went to the side board and poured himself a generous dose of brandy which he self administered immediately patted his belly and waddled over to the table of maps. "I expect Heracles to be here sometime tomorrow if things work out as planned," he mumbled to himself. "Let me see," as he located Dumfries on the map and ran the tip of his forefinger to Aquia Landing and then down to Fredericksburg ending in Richmond. "Yes, tomorrow by early afternoon. Act one ends and the intermission begins. It will be a short one with much scenery, many props and a few actors to be moved into position in preparation for Act two. My trip to meet and recruit the great general George Brinton McClellan. I can't wait, in fact I can't wait for the delivery of my telegram's response." He went to the door, opened it and said to his office staff, as he rushed by them, "I'm going to the telegraph office."

DUMFRIES TO RICHMOND

Hill was granted freedom of the camp which was on the south side of town. A one story, two rooms wooden shed-like structure with an uncovered porch was headquarters. It stood like a lonely grey sentinel in a small sea of white canvas tents. The troops had the tents and the horses had a coral under the spread of some ancient oaks. That is where Hill was found sitting on the fence brushing Champ when a trooper ran up, saluted and requested his presence at headquarters. Hill climbed down asked the trooper to see that Champ was saddled and brought up to headquarters. "I think we'll be taking a little ride real soon, " he said, returned the trooper's salute and executed a quick march to headquarters. The Major, emerging from the shed, stepped off the porch, came to attention, saluted and held out a single page document to Hill. The salute was returned, the document accepted and Hill read it. He smiled, folded it and placed it in his blouse pocket. "Thank you Major," and he extended his hand to shake that of his former captor now host and servant. "I must be on my way without delay." Champ had arrived and Hill received the reins, patted Champ's neck producing an all too familiar and welcome whicker.

"I am at your service, sir, I'll arrange an escort immediately and we'll be on our way to Aquia Station post-haste," responded the major with an element of waried respect.

Hill had his boots and socks off for the first time since he left Alexandria. He was reclined against the stall wall sitting on a clump of hay as Champ was making a meal of some oats. As usual he preferred the car for horses and that particular facility on the Richmond, Fredericksburg and Potomac line was fit for champions and there was Champ enjoying his due. Hill rehashed the events of the past couple of days, a living nightmare that appears to be ending well with his anticipated meeting with Secretary Benjamin. He thought of Nel and longed for her and an immediate sting of conscience stabbed his daydream...the picture of his loving and loyal wife tending the home fires in anticipation of his return. Damn, he thought, I suffer the curse of the Hill men.

There was a short delay in Fredericksburg and he dozed most of the way to Richmond. Upon arrival there he rode Champ at a trot to the War Department a number of blocks away at ninth and Bank streets. He tied up Champ and ran up the steps past clerks, officers and orderlies and stopped short of the oaken door to the Secretary's office. "Is he in?" he asked the orderly and with an abruptness commanded, "Tell him Heracles is here and tell him now despite who is with him." The orderly left his desk, knocked three times on the oaken door opened it and disappeared behind it. In seconds the door burst open revealing a flushed, smiling Judah Benjamin with his arms extended in front of his rotund middle. "My dear Colonel, my darling boy, come in, come in," as he advanced and gave an unembarrassed bear hug to Hill who was embarrassed. The two entered the office and the orderly closed the door only to have it opened immediately by Benjamin who ordered not to be disturbed except for a feast of roast beef, baked ham, corn bread, yams and a bucket of butter in one hour and he slammed the door.

Benjamin led Hill to the two chairs by the hearth, they each sat, Benjamin and Hill, both on the edge of their seats. The Secretary couldn't wait, leaning forward with hands extended and palms up, "Is our Target ready and the scene set for my grand entrance from stage right?"

"Yes and in fours, your Excellency, he's not only ready and anxious for your visit, I feel he's ready to accept our proposal as his noblesse oblige." Hill sat back in his chair with a look of complete satisfaction that was perceived as such by Benjamin.

"Splendid indeed," was Judah's responsive remark as he left his chair, advanced to the sideboard, poured a hefty portion from the crystal decanter of Napoleon Brandy into two snifters and approached Hill. He gave one snifter to Hill and raised his. "To our new Little Napoleon...our Bonaparte," emphasizing the "our." They both took healthy swigs of the nectar of Mars. "There will come a time for me to hear of the details of your adventure in enemy country---and our own," and he chuckled. "Alas now we must ignite this part of our engine of war from the sparks you have produced. All props and actors are in place and their lines and roles memorized. It is now time to raise the curtain for act II. Nelly, dentist Van Camp and hotelier Green, will be notified by a courier's verbal message, nothing in writing, that the general's toothache will occur exactly 5 days from now. The French delegation will proceed to Washington via the R.F.&P. rail road to Aquia Station and from there by carriages to Alexandria, where I leave their party. The party leaves Richmond at dawn three days from now, allowing two days of travel to reach D.C.. Personally I know that is a bit excessive in estimation; we will be there in a day. I plan to spend no more than three hours with the general and return by hearse through the lines later that afternoon. I'll transfer to a fast carriage and overnight in Woodbridge or Dumfries, then on to Aquia for the R. F. & P. line to Richmond. Thus the curtain falls on Act II.

Base to Target

Judah sat in the parlor car with the Consul General's party but not with the Consul General. He played his role of a French chef, delighting in his ability to display his theatrical talents and Gallic linguistic skills with the maids and valets of the official French entourage and kept a respectable distance from the elite. Even his good friend, Alfred Paul, didn't recognize Benjamin when he joined the party on the platform of the railroad station in Richmond. This pleased Judah immensely and appealed to his latent thespian streak. The train ride to Aquia Station was uneventful. From there a small convoy of six coaches carried the party north, escorted by a military escort of Virginia Militia Cavalry to a point just south of the Alexandria town limits. There, by prior arrangement, they were met by a contingent of Union Cavalry, to be escorted to the French Embassy in Washington, D.C. Actually, McClellan considered meeting the official French party but thought better of it and sent a new brevet brigadier general instead. Consul Paul had been briefed by Benjamin to stall the party in the center of town in Alexandria. Some food and drink in a place other than a bare board road house where chef Jean Paul could inspect the kitchen and slip out the back door to make his way to Dr. Van Camp's operatory.

Dr Aaron Van Camp was a bit anxious upon Benjamin's arrival. He had been expecting it according to his briefing but he developed a case of nerves awaiting the Secretary's arrival. And when that moment came, it was met with mixed feelings. He was pleased and proud that he was able to be a part of such an important event but he was well aware of the imminent danger of catastrophic consequences if the plot was discovered by the Union spies that were in abundance in and about Alexandria. Benjamin was a charming and cooperative guest. He was ushered into Van Camp's private office, with curtains drawn, behind the operatory where Benjamin Franklin Stringfellow, a fellow spy in the Greenhow Ring, was working on a wide-mouthed patient as Dr. Van Camp's dental assistant.

No sooner had the secretary doffed his long cape, removed the false full grey beard, handlebar mustache and long grey wig when there was some excitement in the street in front of the dentist's office. Van Camp, alarmed, told Benjamin to remain in the private office with the door closed and locked, only to be opened in response to 4 knocks, a pause and 3 knocks on the door. Van Camp went into the operatory and Benjamin reached for his pocketed flask, found a glass tumbler and poured 3 fingers of brandy. "Here's to the Confederacy and a successful expedition," he whispered and took a healthy belt of the liquor.

On the other side of the door, the excitement in the street evolved into excitement in the office. It seems, according to the Union Captain who identified himself as General McClellan's aide in an abrupt manner, that the general had been seized by a sudden excruciating face pain, so severe and disabling that he was unable to continue his inspection tour with his staff and escort. "He was swooning...the doctor must see the general immediately."

Van Camp agreed and told his assistant to clear out the waiting room and get ready for the general. But the captain had already cleared the office of patients and had the general carried into the operatory. McClellan's affect was appropriate. He appeared limp-limbed and offered subdued moans each one of which caused his aide to show visible signs of sympathetic pain. Van Camp helped the general out of his blouse and into the chair; the aide had already taken his saber and handled it like it was the holy grail. Other officers started appearing, crowding the place. Van Camp suddenly shouted, "Out, all of you, out this instant. This is a temple of mercy and comfort. Allow this poor man his due of courtesy, decency and privacy. Allow me to do my blessed work." In silence the mob dispersed into the waiting room. The captain remained at the door. "Captain, you will be the interlocutor. When I am finished, I will report to you my findings, treatment and further orders. Have a seat by this door and let no one enter. This door is not to open until I open it. Understood?" Van camp scowled at the captain.

"Very well sir," responded the aide who appeared in need of the chair and soon. Van Camp closed and locked the door to the operatory. He approached the recumbent figure in the chair who was coming out of it as soon as he heard the latch fall in the door lock. His extended hand was received by that of the dentist. No word was spoken. Van Camp went to the door of his private office, knocked 4 times, paused then thrice and the door opened.

Enter Spy Mistress Blue

Things were pacific, as they usually were on the sedate Church Hill of Richmond. It was hot, sticky and quiet. Nothing was astir but a now-and-then slight humid breeze moved up the slope from the James River that offered no relief from the dog days discomfort. But at the stately Van Lew mansion on Grace Street something was astir. Elizabeth Van Lew was in a stew. Something had to be done in the mad and maddening city, the capital of the Confederacy. Miss Van Lew was a 43-year-old wealthy, socialite spinster, living with her widowed mother in the family mansion, as a known Union sympathizer in the heart of the Confederacy. What was not known was that she was a Union spy and a very effective one at that. The Van Lew mansion was a hub of espionage for the Union from the start and throughout the entire war years. Her farm outside Richmond was a sub-station of her communication system to Washington. She vetted, recruited, trained and ran her own network of informants and couriers that went from the planning desks of the War Department and the very desk of President Jefferson Davis to the eyes only of President Abraham Lincoln and Generals Benjamin Butler and later, U.S. Grant.

Aside from her own network, which grew including John Minor Botts, a lawyer, farmer and former Congressman, F. W. E. Lohman, a grocer, William Rowley, a farmer and William Fay, a carpenter. Among the female collaborators were Eliza Carrington, a friend, Varina Davis' seamstress who went unidentified and Josephine Holmes, a daughter of a member of the underground. She collaborated with other Union sympathizers and spies in Richmond like Samuel Ruth, the railroad superintendent and

Thomas McNiven, the baker who supplied the Grey House with breads and pastries.

Despite their eternal vigilance, persistent surveillance and multiple attempts at entrapment, the detectives, ("the plug-uglies," as they were ungratefully known by the citizens of Richmond) of General John Winder, Provost Marshal of Richmond, failed to discover any substantial evidence of her aiding and abetting the enemy. She was the queen bee of the hidden hive of huggermugger, espionage, marshaling her growing swarm of worker bees, spies, sitting atop Church Hill in plain sight of the seat of government of the C.S.A.. Among her amazing, daring and unbelievable accomplishments was the placement of Mary Jane Richards Bowser, her former servant, a freed slave, as a maid in the Confederate White House. Remarkably, Mary Jane had been a favorite of Elizabeth's and was sent north to a Quaker school in Princeton, New Jersey. She was called back to Church Hill by her benefactor for things; actions and events that were extraordinaire. Miss Elizabeth wanted her to be a spy...and not just a run-of-the-mill, back alley dissembler but a spy in the household of the President of the Confederate States of America, His Excellency, Jefferson Davis.

Mary Jane was not only literate but she was eidetic; she could memorize what she read, remember it to be recorded in toto at a later time in a secure setting to be transmitted to Miss Elizabeth for delivery north. She was to conduct herself in the Grey House, as an illiterate not very bright slave girl, "obsequious in manner and bumbling in speech," who had trouble making eye contact with the adult white folk but "Ahs gets on good wit da younguns."

Mary Jane had married Wilson Bowser, another of Elizabeth Van Lew's servants, a freed man, who was placed at the Van Lew vegetable farm outside Richmond where he oversaw the first outstation of Elizabeth's sub rosa line of communication north. He was also instrumental in recruiting slaves and freedmen in Miss Elizabeth's efforts to preserve the Union and eventually free the slaves once the Emancipation Proclamation was established and followed by Lincoln's armies.

Judah Benjamin was beyond his bombast by now and was assuming a more pedestrian approach with his favorite marshal of men and champion of ideals, the new Napoleon. Time for an extended pause for dramatic effect. Their entire meeting was conducted in French. McClellan was enthralled by the oratory, mesmerized by the rhetoric, entranced by the unquestioned logic and unassailable reason that this great man, steeped in the classics and armed with the wisdom of the ages, had preceded this recess...a welcome pause for both.

McClellan left his chair, strode to the window and parted the curtains just enough to get a peek at the alley behind the office. Some of his escort were milling about, off their mounts, demonstrating subtle but poorly disguised expressions of boredom. His staff, those who remained, were out front sending couriers with orders for the troops conducting military business as usual, waiting with evident impatience for their commander to appear whole and relieved of his misery. Dr. Van Camp had informed the general's aide-de-camp. "The molar extraction was successful but was complicated by bleeding from the socket that's flow was difficult to staunch. Perhaps the captain would be so kind to obtain the use of an ambulance to carry the general to his quarters when he is discharged in about two hours." The Captain was quick to respond and gave the orders for the ambulance. Dr. Van Camp returned to his operatory and locked the door. In a cold sweat he collapsed into the dental chair and prayed for a quick and quiet end to this adventure.

In the room behind the operatory Judah Benjamin poured a generous portion of brandy into both crystal tumblers, raised his, as did McClellan, they clinked and Benjamin toasted. "To our future of the perpetuity..perpetuity..of peace, prosperity and preservation of our land..our land.. and life as God has granted and to you..you.. his appointed guarantor."

McClellan smiled, raised his tumbler, they clinked again and the general responded, "God willing as am I, so be it!"

"And now my general, it is time to leave the lovely language of nobility, return to our mundane roles on the rude boards of life's little stages enforced and enlivened by our knowledge and acceptance of our communal noblesse oblige." And he thought to himself, let the curtain rise on Act III.

Their ethereal mood was interrupted by a sudden disturbance in the street in front of the office. It seems the ambulance arrived just before a hearse drove up. Alarm spread through the military escort and staff. The general's aide, beside himself, rushed up to the black driver of the hearse, telling the ambulance attendants to be at ease, and demanded of Joshua the black hearse driver, his business. Joshua stated, "Ahs to picks up a departed from this address." And he offered the captain a note with Dr. Van Camp's home address on it stating the deceased, Alexander Van Camp, an 85 years old male, was to be collected and delivered to the Sullivan Funeral Parlor for funeral preparation. The captain told Joshua to stay put until he returned and ran into the dentist's waiting room with his ambulance attendants close on his heels.

In the meantime, Dr. Van Camp, in a flash, had sized up the situation in danger of becoming a calamity. He sent Judah Benjamin up the stairs to the living quarters, got the general into the dental chair in the operatory, ordered his assistant to wrap a large white bandage about the general's jaw and opened the door to the near apoplectic captain. He was pale and sweating as was the dentist.

"What in hell is going on Dr.?" he barked, "My troops think the general is dead," as he crooked his neck to look over Van Camp's shoulder at the body in the dental chair, getting a bandage wrapped around his head.

"Well, captain, you can see for yourself that the general is alive and well." At that point McClellan waved his right hand and spoke. "I am ready to leave," delivered in a parade ground tone. He got up from the chair and the two ambulance men moved to his either side to offer assistance which he rapidly refused. The aide went for the general's blouse and sword. "The doctor ordered the ambulance for you sir. I think it best you take it,“ as he snapped to attention and saluted.

"What say you Dr. Van Camp?" McClellan asked.

"I'd request you take the ambulance sir, the blood loss and chloroform effects you know." replied the dentist.

"Your assistant told me of your most recent loss of your beloved father. I offer my condolence and deepest sympathy and heartfelt apology for interfering in your time of grief. And of course my most sincere gratitude for your blessed attendance to my acute needs. What do I owe you for your rendered services?" McClellan reached into his trouser pocket.

"You owe me nothing sir, it was my honor, privilege and pleasure to serve our cause." the dentist smiled and told his assistant to tell the driver to take the hearse to the rear door in the alley.

The general and his party left. Dr. Van Camp went into the back room, locked the door, poured what was left of the brandy into one of the half empty tumblers used by the previous guests and in a sweat soaked clinical cloak collapsed into the Windsor chair still warm from the corpulent rear end of Judah Benjamin.

Stringfellow, Van Camp, Joshua and two of the network heavies brought in the special casket, out fitted with vent holes in the head, which was a hinged separate part of the lid so as to view only the deceased's head. There was a well padded mattress, three silk pillows and a quilt with two bottles of Napoleon brandy, a crystal tumbler and a few French pastries with a folded linen napkin. "Fit for a king," remarked Stringfellow and chuckled.

Van Camp frowned, "We must make haste, friends are waiting in Lorton." He climbed the stairs to the living room above the office and found Benjamin reclining in a wingback chair.

"Everything is ready your Excellency; I trust you are," he was able to verbalize with a slight stammer. Benjamin rose from the chair gave a slight nod and, what Van Camp thought was a suggestion of a smile. "Please sir, allow me the distinct pleasure to extend to you my most sincere appreciation for laboring for one not so foolish to be ungrateful. Lead on." They both descended the steps.

Benjamin surveyed the scene, approached the open casket, took from it a bottle of Napoleon, uncorked it, poured 4 fingers into the waiting tumbler, turned to all present, raised his tumbler, "To a heavenly journey." and emptied the tumbler. He needed the assistance of Stringfellow to remove his boots and was lifted into the conveyance by the two network men. The lids were closed, Van Camp tapped twice on the upper lid, "Are you comfortable?" he asked with his face close to the lid. A muffled, "I am heavenly, let us be on our way," eased the anxiety of the quasi- funeral guests.

The casket was carried outside by the pallbearers and placed inside the hearse to the uncovered heads of the few remaining troopers showing their respect for the deceased. Joshua climbed into his seat and was off to Lorton, Virginia, across the line by 20 miles of good road. The rest of the funeral party dispersed. The two network men went about their business and dental assistant and his boss re-entered the back room. As Stringfellow was closing the door, Van Camp was reaching for a fresh bottle of brandy. “Saints be praised,” he kept mumbling to himself, “Cancel all of tomorrow’s appointments,” he ordered his assistant.

Discomfort of the Deceased

Meanwhile, as planned, Joshua was informing the corporal of Union cavalry at a guard post on the line that the deceased died of some pox or plague that was "ketchy." And to the question of, "What is your business down south?" He responded, "Ahs gonna takes im to his kin folk's grave yard in Lorton."

"Pass on," ordered the corporal, "but don't tell them Reb sentries at their line about it bein ketchy; mebbe they can git a dose and save us a few lead balls." and he laughed. Joshua laughed, touched his hat brim and moved out. Judah Benjamin couldn't hear the verbal exchange; he could only imagine what was taking place. When the hearse started to move, he offered a sigh of relief and a short prayer of thanksgiving followed by a chuckle.

This padding and pillows, despite the silk covered down fill are not nearly as accommodating as I had expected nor informed, thought a not so comfortable Secretary of War as he discovered his confines to be so limited that he was unable to change his position from the supine. Joshua couldn't open the head end of the casket until past the next and last checkpoint which announced their entry into friendly country. Oh for that to come and soon. He felt for the bottle of brandy and brought it up and placed it on the pillow next to his head. The calves of his legs were beginning to cramp and his toes were getting numb. His discomfort and displeasure were increasing by the minute. He uncorked the brandy bottle and tried to get the mouth of the bottle into his mouth but before those mouths could unite a golden stream of brandy belched forth striking his cheek and breaking into multiple rivulets of the nectar. They coursed through the creases and crevices of Benjamin's jowls and the interstices of his beard hairs. A trickle made it onto his tongue and he choked. So much for that effort, he thought, and corked the bottle. But he suddenly noticed the hearse had stopped. "Thank the great Jehovah, we are in the land of Dixie," he said aloud.

Joshua failed to comply with the wishes of that "damn yankee horse soldier" and told the Confederate sentry the same rehearsed story and got the same response. "Pass on!" commanded the soldier and away he drove. Time to get the corpse a breath of fresh air, thought the driver as he brought the hearse into a glade of roadside trees, reined in the horses, climbed into the back of the wagon and lifted the head door of the casket lid. The corpse was alive but barely.

Judah Benjamin, through a brandy stained beard, groaned, "Get me out of here you black devil," and the groan changed into a bark, "and be fast about or I'll damn your black ass into the eternal black flames of hell!"

That black devil unfastened the rest of the lid and helped the fat and almost limp Judah Benjamin out of his wooden prison. "Ahs doin ma best fer you Mars Judah, we's almost home," replied Joshua and offered a forced teethy smile.

Benjamin reached for that bottle and poured four fingers of brandy into the tumbler. He emptied the glass in two gulps. " We must be on to Lorton. I will overnight there and get a good night of undisturbed slumber before the carriage ride to Aquia Station. You will return the hearse to Alexandria as soon as I get situated in Lorton. Now let us proceed to lovely Lorton."

Later that night, in a four-poster with clean and fresh bed linens and pillow cases Judah Benjamin luxuriated. The madam of the household had provided a pleasant scent of lilac in the bedroom undisplaced by the soft breeze coming through the open but shuttered window. Before I doze off, I will force a mental recounting of my meeting with McClellan...... something I was unable to accomplish, even attempt, while confined and tortured in that bouncing and jarring coffin causing me cerebral commotion let alone physical insult. But now I can analyze and appreciate, no, rejoice, over the great accomplishment, a heroic achievement that I struck with that little man...that embryonic emperor, the self-anointed "Little Napoleon." And Benjamin laughed aloud. I must control my emotions, he chastised himself, my hostess, if she hears me, will think I've lost my good senses and become detached from my sanity...and he gave a slight chuckle, muffled by the bedclothes pulled up over his mouth. I did enjoy the French, that was an absolute delight to converse and think in that most beautiful of all human utterances. The brandy was good but the pastries were a poor excuse for Parisian. His conceit was all but intolerable but he succumbed to my broadside of oratory and rhetoric. "I did myself proud!" he mumbled to himself as he sat up in bed and chuckled. " I don't think humor is an arrow in that warrior's quiver."

It was evident to me from the start, Benjamin cogitated, that McClellan was well-briefed and prepared for our setup which turned into a celebration of our collaboration. I had little need to expend any significant pressure to achieve my goal which turned out to be our goal. He had already made up his mind as a result of the splendid, well thought out and executed preparatory efforts of A.P. and Nelly. Marvelous! He was most impressed when I announced his favorite first cousin, Henry Brainerd McClellan, enlisted in the 3rd Cavalry Regiment of Virginia on 14 June, 1861. He knew we had investigated him in a most detailed and thorough manner. He was most delighted in the effortless, elementary, and flawless modus operandi of our scheme....he merely keeps writing, as usual, a daily detailed missive to his beloved Nelly who sends it to Abigail who sends it to Jules who copies it to me and sends the original back to Abigail who returns it to Nelly. Simply elegant espionage, he thought and smiled. And if I have a message for "le clarion d'argent," his new nom d'espionage which he admired for its ring and preferred it to that of "Target," I will use secret ink on a blank sheet of stationery that accompanies the return document to Nelly. She will know to forward that blank sheet to le clarion d'argent and he will know to treat it, read it and burn it. I'm a genius. Benjamin got out of bed, relived himself in the chamber pot, returned to bed and fell fast asleep dreaming not of sugar plums but of dearest Jules.

The next morning's road to Aquia Church was sun-drenched and swept by warm, dust-laden breezes rendering the Secretary a sweltering corpulent mass of discomfort in the back of the pre-arranged two horse carriage. The ride was, otherwise, uneventful and his arrival at the connecting point for the R.F.& P. Rail-Road was expected and accommodated without incident. His train ride was the most comfortable of his various means of transport so far although he thought he deserved his own private rail car which he failed to arrange. Two of his staff, a colonel and a major, met him at Fredericksburg and brought him a packet of documents, letters, reports, requests and a list of officers, politicians and vendors seeking a personal audience. His clerk, L.Q. Washington, had arranged them in what he considered, order of importance. He received the packet with an element of displayed displeasure and grumbled, "Here is my living nightmare of that hurricane of papers." The two officers exchanged a fleeting glance of dismay. Checking on him later, they found him dozing among his stilled hurricane of papers and left him undisturbed until they reached the outskirts of Richmond.

At the station he was met by his carriage and a small escort of cavalry whom he directed to take him to his quarters not the War Department. "I've had enough of official and unofficial tomfoolery in the past few days to last a lifetime." he hissed through clenched teeth. No happier group of people than the coachman and troopers witnessed Judah Philip Benjamin go through the portal of Davenport House into the arms of an even happier person, dearest Jules. But Judah was the happiest of the lot. He was home, safe and sound, in one piece and in the arms of his beloved.

THE MIRACLE MISSIVE...E PLURIBUS UNUM

Ten days later, Jules St. Martin, with Clerk Washington trying to hold him back, pulling on his arm, came bursting through the Secretary's oaken door. Benjamin was startled and rose from his desk. "What in blazes is stirring?" he barked. Washington released Jules and said, "He said, 'this can't wait. I must see the Secretary immediately.' and he rushed by me to your door. Terribly sorry sir."

"Please get hold of yourself and resume your place. I will attend to this matter privately," Benjamin responded and held the door for the clerk who departed in haste. Jules was rubbing the arm the clerk had grabbed. In that hand he waved a letter at Benjamin and exclaimed in a loud and excited voice, in French, "Here my dearest Judah is the first product of le clarion d'argent. I just came from the post center and ran straight to you with it."

Benjamin took the letter from Jules, walked to his desk, sat down, reached for his letter opener which was a miniature cavalry saber, unsheathed it and unsealed the missive. A broad smile crossed his face as he savored the sight before him. Here it was...success. His grand scheme, his own, the grandest of all times, in all history was unfolding before his very eyes. The commanding general of the opposition forces at the end of a gold chain in my waistcoat pocket like my gold Swiss pocket watch. Inconceivable but true.

Before he read it, there was some necessary protocol to be addressed, some needed housekeeping to be done. "Dearest

Jules," he declared, "may I remind you that at work we speak only English and when you address me, which should be an infrequent occurrence, you should use 'Excellency' or 'Mr. Secretary.' Your demeanor here at the War Department must always be in accord with military courtesy, discipline and protocol without exception. We must not give the naysayers, of which there are scores, ammunition or evidence for their oh-so-ready charges of favoritism or nepotism. Hark now, I must read this epistle, make my notes in French, and give you the original letter to be copied exactly; every comma, every abbreviation, and even the misspelled word, error in grammar and punctuation....exactly as is. Then I must see both the original and the copy, which I keep and you send the original letter in whatever form or vehicle it arrived by return post to Mrs. Wallingford who will send it back to Nelly." He sat back, glanced toward the ceiling, a soft smile crossed his lips which then spoke. "Its beauty is its simplicity and its simplicity is its security." Benjamin then proceeded to read his first work product of his espionage coup. Jules, awestruck, stood silent and motionless near by.

Amid a few grunts, Benjamin devoured each word, those of endearment to Nelly, the grumblings regarding the obstructions of the aging General Scott, the shortcomings of Lincoln and the disappointments of the Cabinet. "Oh if only I could publish some of this in some of the northern press," he spoke aloud. "A glimpse of the mendacity, the nefarious machinations and rampant corruption within the hallowed halls of the Union government would convey a universal climate of no confidence among the electorate." He glanced at Jules who nodded, approving and smiling.

"Alas, in as much as I would be so inclined by my emotional mind, my rational mind requires me to exercise the maximum discretion in disseminating gained intelligence. In fact I must be exquisitely certain of protecting my most secret source by selecting what information goes to what general. Nothing must be relayed that can identify the source which must be cloaked in secrecy and enshrouded in subterfuge. The highest level of secrecy must be exercised by any and all of those who handle this Silver Bugle material." He held Jules in his gaze. "The integrity and trustworthiness of even you, my dearest Jules and your clerk assistant, co-copier, the staff officer chosen for the task of receiving, analyzing, editing and distributing only that intelligence necessary to the appropriate general officer by one of three examined couriers who would deliver only verbal reports to that commander..all of you in that sacred and secret fraternity must be of unblemished allegiance and unquestioned loyalty."

The electrical silence was broken by a knock at the door. Clerk Washington, stuck his head in and announced, "General Lee is here to see you sir, as appointed."

"Splendid!" remarked Benjamin, "and the timing couldn't be better. By all means, show him in him and ask the porter to bring us some inviting delicacies and accommodating beverages." He rose from behind his desk and went to greet the general as Lee broached the doorway. Jules slipped out as he swept in.

Benjamin's fixed smile/smirk was transformed into a genuine and warm full smile, as he extended his hand. "General Lee, my good fellow, what a Godsend you are."

Lee, immaculate and splendid in uniform, courtly in demeanor, gave a slight bow and accepted the hand of Benjamin. "A venerable privilege to be received in your chambers your Excellency. For what matter am I deserving of such an honor?" responded the general.

Benjamin directed Lee to one of the armchairs by the fireplace and went to the hunt table, reaching for the decanter of brandy. "The sun is over the yardarm General, may I offer you some of Napoleon's nectar of war?"

Lee smiled. “Most kind of your Excellency but I don’t imbibe intoxicants while on duty.”

“But you are not on duty now,,, not in my theater of operation,” and the Secretary of War fortified two Claret stemware with brandy and offered one to Lee, who took it. Benjamin raised his glass and offered a toast, “To victory, Vive la Confederate States of America.” Lee rose to his full military height, clinked the Secretary’s glass and replied, ”God willing” and they both drank.

“Now to the matter at hand General Lee.” And Secretary of War, Judah Philip Benjamin initiated his briefing of General Robert Edward Lee, chief military advisor to Jefferson Finis Davis, President of the Confederate States of America. The session, interrupted once only by the arrival of food and wine, lasted 90 minutes; 60 minutes of exposition and 30 minutes of questions and discussion. It was an exhaustive ordeal for Lee but he was at once attentive, fascinated, intrigued and obsessed with the details as only an engineer would be. Despite his rigid analysis he found no flaw and accepted his role of the clearing house for all the intelligence, maintaining the security of its source and determining and effecting its select distribution to the appropriate commanders. A monumental undertaking indeed, he thought, the masterpiece of an evil genius and, no doubt, Judah Benjamin answers the call and fits the bill. But I can, must and will obey.

“I am duly impressed and compliment your Excellency on your brilliant accomplishment, your creative mentation, your vision... absolutely astounding. I am honored and proud to be chosen for such a mission of majesty. Thank you and God bless you sir.” Lee saluted, reached for his brandy, raised it and toasted, “Vive la Confederate States of America.”

Benjamin responded and pointed to the waiting repast. “Let us satiate our elephantine rumblings of the gut.” They sat, they ate and they were satisfied.

THE PEEP HOLE

Within 2 weeks of daily missives, occasionally more than one a day, it became apparent that Jules was overwhelmed and so was dearest brother Judah. So Jules hollered for help and Judah responded. Word went out from the War Department that a clerk for the Secretary's office was sought who was not only literate but schooled and a master of grammar and rhetoric and was gifted in penmanship. In no time Elizabeth Van Lew was apprised of the situation by her source at the War Department and she lost no time in sifting through her mental file of agents for a suitable candidate. Most of her agents were adults and some of advanced age, not eligible for the military draft; those age appropriate were destined for military service. That left a search for a young male not of military age who was literate, intelligent and who had unquestioned loyalty to Elizabeth Van Lew's views on preservation of the Union at any cost. She found such a one in the person of James McNiven, a teenage son of Thomas McNiven, an accomplished and trusted operator within his own and Van Lew's network. Arrangements were made, James was briefed on his role and his interview was scheduled...and with none other than Jules St. Martin. How sweet! And that's exactly how Jules described young James to Benjamin.

"He is such a sweet and beautiful boy," expressed Jules, "he and I will get along, c'est extraordinaire. His penmanship is that of a medieval monk."

"But can he keep a secret?" queried Benjamin.

"Oh dearest Judah I exercised grave concern in expressing how honored and privileged he'd be to be working in the very shadow of the Secretary of War and how sacred the secrets we were to behold and must hold dear and protect from unauthorized exposure. Not even your family must know of what we are about. He gave me his word of honour. He is golden dearest Judah. He is to report to me tomorrow at 9:00 A.M."

"Carry on Jules but keep both your eyes and thumbs on him."

Le Clarion D'Argent, Its Joyful Noise

George Brinton McClellan, Commanding General, as was his wont, continued to generate disaffection and friction among powerful newspaper editors, Cabinet members, influential Congressman and Senators and disappointment with his immediate superiors, War Secretaries, first Cameron then Stanton and President Lincoln. He tolerated Cameron, regarded Secretary of the Navy, Gideon Welles as an old woman, Attorney General Bates as an old fool and Secretary of State Seward as a meddling, officious and incompetent little puppy. And all of his displeasure was conveyed in great detail by daily letters (and telegrams later) to dear Nelly ...and, of course, to his Excellency, Judah Benjamin and eventually to General Lee. Benjamin drooled over the disparaging remarks and negative gossip McClellan provided..best of all was his reference to Lincoln as a gorilla. This evoked a loud guffaw from the sedate Secretary of War. But Lee edited out the non-military drivel in his analyses sent to the field commanders.

Lieutenant General Winfield Scott, General-in-Chief of the Union Army forwarded a plan that was dubbed the "Anaconda Plan," which entailed blockade of the major Atlantic and Gulf ports of the South and an aggressive expedition down the Mississippi River to New Orleans, splitting the Confederacy and strangling it into submission. "Little Napoleon" would have none of it...nor would Benjamin. In fact, McClellan would tolerate his general-in-chief not much longer. To Nelly he wrote, "...how can I save this country when stopped by Genl Scott---I do not know whether he is a dotard or a traitor! I am leaving nothing undone to increase our force---but that confounded old Genl always comes in the way---he is a perfect imbecile. He understands nothing, appreciates nothing & is ever in my way." It was a given fact that McClellan would win out; on 1 November 1861, he was notified that Lincoln had designated him "to command the whole Army."

McClellan's plan was grand, "The Urbanna Plan." He would attack Richmond, the capital of the Confederacy 75 miles south of D.C. by crow flight, but not by marching south across northern Virginia. There, he agued, the enemy's forces would be laying in wait in vast numbers, well supplied, on familiar ground and battle-hardened. Rather, he'd execute a martial exercise the likes of which the world had never beheld. Rather than unleashing an invasion entirely overland and along the path expected by the enemy, he'd take his army on a 180 miles journey, 130 by water and 50 by land, down the Potomac River from Alexandria, Virginia into the Chesapeake Bay to Urbanna, Virginia, a spot on the Rappahannock River. There he'd disembark his forces and march across 50 miles of good sandy roads west to Richmond, outflanking General Joseph E. Johnston's Confederates in their works at Bull Run and Centrevlle. It was a good plan and his generals all agreed. And so did Benjamin and Lee; for it would provide valuable time to prepare for the Union's invasion. Information of the secret grand plan reached the eyes of Benjamin and Lee through the Silver Bugle's letters to Nelly and eventually to the ears of General Joe Johnston. Lee advised Johnson to vacate his works at Manassas and to regroup below the Rappahannock River. This was accomplished within twenty-four hours sub rosa, leaving McClellan unaware until Lincoln ordered him to advance on the Confederates at Bull Run. His probing forces found the fortifications abandoned. So much for the grand Urbanna Plan. In disappointment an alternative plan was developed. Instead of Urbanna it would be Fortress Monroe, 150 miles by water, at Hampton Roads on the tip of the peninsula between the James and the York Rivers. The army would disembark there and march up the peninsula 70 miles to Richmond, using the navy to protect his flanks with their gunboats in the James and York Rivers. But the C.S.S. Virginia, the former U.S.S. Merrimac converted into an iron-clad marauding warship changed McClellan's plans again. He could no longer plan on using the James River because the C.S,S. Virginia blocked its entrance. So after an inordinate time of planning and preparation that delineated a sharp line between his political foes and friends in Washington, (it pleased Judah Benjamin and General Lee because of the time it granted the Confederates to marshal their defenses), McClellan set sail from Alexandria on the steamer Commodore arriving at Fort Monroe in the late afternoon of 2 April, 1862. It was among the other 400 steamers, barges and schooners loaded with troops, horses, cannons, mortars, siege guns, wagons and supplies that anchored in the waters around Fort Monroe. It was a sight to behold. Never before in the history of warfare had such a mass of arms been so transported to do battle.

His plan was to outflank the entrenched Confederates at Yorktown commanded by General James B. Magruder, "Prince John" as he was known. Magruder's caper of showing as many of his troops to Union observers along his lines turned his 11,000 troops into a much larger and menacing force in McClellan's mind and reports. Furthermore, heavy rain turned roads, that were reported earlier to be passable in any weather, into impassable rivers of mud. Lack of maps and current intelligence and discovery that a line of fortifications extended from Yorktown, across the entire peninsula running behind the Warwick River and marshes, to the James River was an unexpected impediment. A change of plans, once again, was in order and with it a delay in action, once again, good news for the War Department in Richmond. McClellan called up the siege train to bombard Yorktown. This coincided with a surprising dispatch from Washington that Lincoln was withholding McDowell's First Corps to protect Washington, not to join McClellan, as planned. McClellan's outrage was matched by Richmond's glee and Lee advised Johnston to withdraw his forces to Williamsburg sub rosa, just like Manassas. The fact that the fortifications of Yorktown had been abandoned reached McClellan on 4 May just before his siege guns were to start the bombardment of Yorktown. On 5 May Johnston's retreating forces, despite losing the battle of Williamsburg, were able to withdraw farther up the peninsula to the banks of the Chickahominy River followed by segments of McClellan's forces, both armies in slow march through the rain and mud. McClellan divided his army into two elements; one on each side of the Chickahominy and Johnston attacked one half of the Union army and lost the battle of Fair Oaks (Seven Pines) on 31 May. During that battle Johnston suffered serious disabling wounds by shot and shell that resulted in Lee assuming command of the forces defending Richmond.

Lee knew, as did Johnston, that Richmond's only defense was an aggressive offense because the Confederate Capital could not withstand a siege offensive that the Union could deliver. So capitalizing on McClellan's forces being split across the Chickahominy Lee seized upon the opportunity to attack General Fitz-John Porter's V Corps on the north side of the Chickahominy with an attempt to cut the Union supply line from its base at White House Landing on the York River. The Seven Days Battles from 25 June through 1 July,1862, including engagements at Oak Grove, Mechanicsville & Beaver Dam Creek, Gaines' Mill, Savage's Station and Malvern Hill were characterized by neither Lee nor McClellan as achieving a decisive tactical victory. McClellan, with forces four miles from Richmond, the Union troops of General Philip Kearny could see the church spires, failed to take the Confederate capital and retreated in a "change of base" after each battle. Although Malvern Hill's battle favored the Union forces, McClellan withdrew from the field as the vanquished rather than the victor. Distraught by this poor generalship, derelict tactics and suspect strategy, General Philip Kearney, one of McClellan's fighting generals, observed to his staff, "His legacy, appropriate for the man, will be relegated to that portion of his anatomy, for which the saddle which bears his name, is designed to receive."

Elizabeth Van Lew was livid. Richmond should be crawling with blue coats, forces of occupation, and the war should be over. But it wasn't and she couldn't fathom the reason why. She knew how critical the domestic situation was and how vulnerable were the Confederate forces in and around Richmond from her sources in the War Department, the Confederate Gray House and her own eyes and ears. What was wrong with General McClellan? Why retreat? Why not attack?

A few blocks away at 9th and Banks streets, Judah Benjamin was ecstatic with the Silver Bugle's skedaddle down the peninsula following the secretary's "directed suggestions," he didn't want to call them "orders." And titillated was he with reading the delicious gossip he obtained from McClellan's ongoing battle by wire with that detestable lot of knaves in Washington. But Lee, even though he saved Richmond, was displeased with his failure to destroy the Union army and for his huge troop loss. However, having analyzed his opponent accurately as an over cautious engineer and not a warrior, Lee maintained the initiative and led his Army of Northern Virginia northward toward Manassas. Before doing so, he delegated his role of analyst, editor and disseminator of the Silver Bugle intelligence product to his aide, the scholarly academic, Major Charles S. Venable.

Lincoln became alarmed for the safety of Washington and directed general-in-chief Halleck to order McClellan to abandon Harrison's Landing with celerity and reform the Army of the Potomac on the Rappahannock Line to reinforce generals Burnside and Pope. The "Little Napoleon" was not pleased but Benjamin was and Lee was informed. The dispatch caused McClellan, "the greatest pain I ever experienced." Benjamin's next secret-inked missive in French to the Silver Bugle was full of flowered and grand compliments and verbal tokens of appreciation and esteem for the military genius exhibited and..may it continue. The Union administration in Washington and military leaders in the field were in delicious chaos and..may that continue was his sign off. McClellan was ambivalent. The silent pleasure derived from his sacred mission with his intellectual visionary compadres in Richmond to preserve the Union falls short of warding off the mounting despair and pain suffered upon him by the beasts in Washington. Nelly was aware of this and countered it by effusive commendatory and laudatory language and expressions of romantic tenderness in her letters to her dearest George. She knew how to manage her George; appeal to his inflated self-image and indelible conceit. Benjamin did also and accentuated the Silver Bugle's noblesse oblige among a deluge of flattery.

Thus, the abandonment of Harrison's Landing was a slow and protracted exercise resulting in the Army of the Potomac failing to reinforce Burnside and Pope in a timely fashion. Consequently the second Battle of Bull Run was just like the first, another embarrassing defeat for the Union forces. The brandy decanter was emptied in the office on the second floor of the War Department in Richmond. In an adjoining restricted and locked office two young men worked in great haste and secrecy copying letters. Jules St. Martin would leave his desk frequently to "confer with the secretary." James, "Little Jimmy" McNiven rarely left his desk not even for lunch, which his mother packed for him each morning and was carried in his lunch pail. In that pail, which was never searched, he sequestered copies of the letters he copied for his excellency Secretary Benjamin, and carried home to his father who delivered them to Elizabeth Van Lew.

Le Clarion D'Argent, A Sour Note

Shocked, appalled, devastated, disheartened, dismayed, dumbstruck...Elizabeth Van Lew was all of these. Her emotional and physical response was profound..."This can't be true; it is loathsome, moral decadence of the lowest caliber not in our loving God's creation. This man is wicked, vile, Beelzebub in Union blue." spoken out loud, seated at her desk in the solitude of her library. She felt a sudden wave of nausea and the blood drain from her face. "Who would give credence to such astounding and startling information?" She rose from her desk, chin in hand, ambled to the mantel and leaned on the carved marble figures with her extended arm, staring into the cold hearth thinking. Her brain was in a state of cerebral commotion. What to do? Whom to tell and how? Our commanding general, guilty of treason. General George Brinton McClellan, a traitor! How tragic! In early June she had expected Richmond to be occupied by Union forces, as had Lincoln, his cabinet and even Jefferson Davis, who sent his wife and children to Raleigh, North Carolina. Elizabeth had arranged in her mansion a "charming chamber, General McClellan's room," for the liberating hero. Tears welled and were damped before they ran down her cheeks with a fine laced linen handkerchief pulled from her sleeve. She returned to her desk, clutched the gnarled ends of the arms of the chair and sat erect in silent and stunned mourning. Before I act, I must confirm this with Mary Jane Bowser, she thought. Now it all makes sense, such sorrowful sense.

Lee had crossed the Potomac it was reported but not confirmed by Pinkerton or Pleasanton. Lincoln wanted to destroy the Confederate Army of Northern Virginia but to keep the Union army between it and Washington in the process. His main problem was who was to lead the Union army in this campaign? He wasn't happy with McClellan and wanted Halleck to take the field but Halleck dodged Lincoln's request and gave the order to McClellan to organize a field army to meet that threat. To McClellan's question as to who would lead that field army he'd organize, Halleck stated that it was not yet decided. However, on 5 September at McClellan's house on H street, he met with Lincoln and Halleck and came away with the notion that he was to lead the army for the Maryland campaign. That afternoon his headquarters issued marching orders to his various commands. McClellan was pleased, Benjamin was pleased, Lee was pleased but Lincoln and Halleck were displeased and worried and Edwin Stanton was outraged. "We must use the tools we have," Lincoln remarked to his secretary, John Hay.

The young Napoleon had the slows pursuing Lee, to Benjamin's delight and in keeping with the secretary's "directed suggestions," advancing only six miles on 12 September. He went not much farther on 13 September when he entered the city of Frederick, Maryland to a hero's welcome. Frederick had been occupied by the Confederates for the prior five days. Later that day soldiers of the 27th Indiana in bivouac found a copy of Lee's Special Orders No 191 in a field where they lay and spirited them up the command to McClellan. He was stunned, first in disbelief, then in delight with such unexpected good fortune. What better gift than your opposing general's plan of action in your own hands? But McClellan, true to form, was what he was; he failed to make the most of his new found intelligence gold mine, didn't inform his senior generals of the find and delayed tactical maneuvers to best his divided foe that would assure a victorious outcome of the Maryland campaign. Harper's Ferry fell into Confederate hands with the surrender and parole of 11,700 Union troops. Lee, with

38,000 men under arms, whose number, in McClellan's mind, was at least 120,000 took up positions on the west bank of the Antietam Creek that emptied into the Potomac River a couple of miles south of Sharpsbug, Maryland. McClelland had 95,000 men of whom 75,000 were rifle-ready who were on the verge of crushing Lee's army near the end of the day on 17 September when A.P. Hill arrived after a forced march from Harper's Ferry and saved the day for the Confederates. It was the bloodiest day in the history of American warfare; the results of the battle were indecisive. Yet McClellan reported it as a victory to Washington stating, "the enemy is driven back into Virginia, Maryland & Penna. are now safe." The efforts of pursuit were lackluster and Washington was furious. Benjamin was pleased but not overjoyed; his army was not crushed but the loss was immense and intolerable. Le Clarion D'argent performed well but by doing so Benjamin was concerned that the persistent rumble of displeasure he generated among Lincoln and his Washington knaves might become a crescendo of thunder with dire consequences including demotion or termination.

Lee withdrew on the night of the 18th and crossed the Potomac back into Virginia with a line of ambulances and wagons 14 miles long carrying 13,724 casualties. The Union losses were 27,000; 11,700 were paroled troops captured by the Confederates at Harpers Ferry. Union casualties were 12,410 and the landscape exploded with hospitals of all kinds and sorts, stables, barns, homes, churches, meeting halls and tents or plain open fields. At one point not only the battlefield but the Antietam Creek ran red.

Judah Benjamin spent most, if not all, of his time in three places, the War Department, the Gray House and the Davenport house. The greatest fraction of time was at the Gray house, where he, as the "Dark Prince" and "Queen Varina" ran the Confederate States of America sub rosa. Jefferson Davis, as mentioned before, suffered an undiagnosed syndrome of recurrent debilitating episodes about which only Varina Davis, Judah Benjamin and a few servants were aware of this malady and its consequences. It was a well kept secret from any and all others. Mary Jane Bowser was one of those aware because of her intimacy of contact with the principals who regarded her, according to the Van Lew plan, as a dull, non verbal, obedient servant who was about "but not quite there." As such she was disregarded when matters of import were discussed. But her demeanor hid her inherent intelligence and eidetic memory which were at constant play and she confirmed to Elizabeth Van Lew the closely guarded secret that McClellan was, in fact, a direct, constant source of information to the Gray House.

THE GRAY CAT IS OUT OF THE BLUE BAG

Miss Van Lew was alone in her library, assessing, pondering, ruminating. Nothing must be committed to paper. None of her operatives could act as courier in relay. Only one courier. This most critical intelligence is so sensitive that it must be conveyed directly to the Commander in Chief, no intermediary, staff or subordinate; to President Abraham Lincoln himself. Elizabeth left her chair and went to the hearth, leaned on the mantel and stared into infinity through the stack of cold logs. And I must be that courier. Nobody but I have the presence and knowledge to convince Mr. Lincoln of the validity of the message I carry to him and him alone. She spoke for the first time. "Tempus fugit and time is of the essence."

The plan, and it worked, was to visit a close cousin who recently suffered a stroke at her home in Ardmore, Maryland, a Washington suburb. She was an only child and a spinster of some wealth with a longtime employed house staff to care for her but Elizabeth was her next of kin and executor of her estate. Elizabeth's presence was required to clarify some administrative concerns. A pass from General John Winder, the Confederate Provost Marshal, to whom she was well known, was no problem and would most assuredly negate the need for any search of luggage or person at the frontier. Selected copies of letters from McClellan to Nelly as unquestioned evidence to support her verbal report were secreted into the folds of her parasol. John Van Lew, Elizabeth's brother, travelled in his business so he made her travel arrangements and accommodations at Willard's Hotel in Washington. She knew that

Lincoln's office was open to the public so she could gain access to him without the need for a sponsor or a pass. Thus she joined the White House visitors seeking an audience with the President in the blue room on the first floor and held back from the mass of people shepherded up to the second floor office where Lincoln received his visitors. She greeted Lincoln as the session drew to a close and spoke' directly into his ear, " I have valuable news from Richmond. Read my note." as she slipped a note into his palm. It read,

> "Most secret and urgent. Your eyes and ears only.
>
> Clandestine immediate meeting a must. Your personal
>
> response only to Elizabeth Van Lew, Rm 302, Willard's.
>
> God save the Union and God Bless you."

Not more than two hours following the Lincoln audience, a messenger arrived at Willard's Hotel and delivered a sealed envelope from the White House directly into Elizabeth's hand. His orders were to wait for a response which she gave after reading the note. "Please tell the sender of the note that Miss Van Lew is most honored and pleased and will be ready and waiting for Mr. Hay's three knocks, a pause and two knocks on my door tomorrow at 5:30 P.M."

The Soldiers' Home

The Riggs Farm, 500 acres of rolling bucolic countryside on the Maryland side of the Potomac River, three miles north of Washington, was acquired by the federal government for the site of the Soldiers' Home for veterans of the Mexican War. The Riggs cottage, on the grounds, was Lincoln's favored retreat from the summer's heat and humidity, the effluvium of the swamp in which the White House was surrounded and the incessant strains of running a government at war on the edge of enemy territory. John Hay, the closest of his two private secretaries, was sitting next to Elizabeth in the carriage as it pulled up to the stone steps to the porch where Lincoln and his aide, Captain David Derickson, were sitting in rockers. They approached the carriage; the captain led and opened the carriage door to assist Miss Van Lew's exit. Lincoln approached her, smiled, gave a slight bow and accepted her extended hand. "Welcome to my bit of paradise, please come in," he said as he led her into the parlor. He directed her to be seated and ordered tea, asked Hay and Derickson to leave the room with an order of not to be disturbed.

"I thank you, Excellency, for this great honor and God given privilege to meet with you and help you preserve our Union." Elizabeth stated as she pulled scissors from her basket, started to open the folds of her parasol and handed the secreted documents to Lincoln. "These are copies of daily letters from General McClellan to his wife. She sent them to an intermediary, her close friend who relayed them to Jules St. Martin in Richmond, a clerk assistant, and brother-in-law, of Secretary of War, Judah Benjamin, and from him to General Lee whose edited versions went to his field commanders. McClellan tells her everything, secrets, political, military and sometimes twice daily. The original letters, after being copied, are sent back through the same route, sometimes with secret requests or "suggested directions" from Benjamin or Lee, in secret writing, to Mrs. McClellan to be sent to her husband as the blank cover sheet for her letters to him. He burns those pages with the secret writing."

Her delivery was interrupted by the arrival of the tea cart with assorted pastries. Silence reigned until the servant left the room. Neither one touched the attractive presentation of refreshments and delectables.

Elizabeth described enough of her operation to the president so he could attach a degree of validity to her story without compromising her network or operatives. Lincoln started reading the letters, raised his eyebrows, shook his head, shifted in his chair and grunted occasionally. Elizabeth sat in silence.

After reading three of the letters he raised his head and said, "I am dumbfounded, dumbstruck, shocked, grievously disappointed... almost in despair! He rose from his chair, "I should have known... what a fool I've been...I risked the nation on him." He went to the hunt table and poured a healthy slug of bourbon into a tumbler, turned, embarrassed that he overlooked Elizabeth, forced a smile and offered her a liqueur which she politely declined. "You have accomplished an astounding feat of discovery that has escaped my own professionals and I and the nation are in your deepest debt. As you have already deemed, this information must be regarded with the utmost secrecy; for the repercussions, if this becomes known to even a few, would be devastating, a catastrophe of immense dimension, the government would fall and the Union would dissolve. How many people know of this?" he asked

Elizabeth, paused a moment in thought, then spoke. "Of those in the government of Richmond I am unaware; however, the nature of the information and its source, a sensible one must assume, must enjoy tightly controlled and limited exposure and handling. Only four people on our side, I included, are in the know and all have sworn an oath of secrecy...and now you." She smiled.

"My advice to you dear lady is to return to your home, change nothing in your daily routine and tell no one... no one... of your travels and our visit." he spoke with a tone of solemn conviction. "Now let us dine and then send you back to Willards. I must consider my next steps." During dinner, few words were spoken and little food was eaten by either. Lincoln emptied two tumblers of bourbon. "Please inform in detail what we discussed with Mr. John Hay on your ride back to Willards. He is the most privy and trusted of my staff and will be one of the only two people besides me in government who will be aware of our secret." His order was obeyed in the carriage ride into Washington and John Hay was visibly shaken by her briefing. As he departed her rooms at the hotel, she grabbed his arm, fixed his gaze and reminded him, "Remember, not a word to anybody about me, my visit or our secret."

"Most assured Madam." he replied and strode down the hall. left the hotel and entered the carriage for the ride back to the cottage at the Soldiers' Home.

Two evenings later, Abraham Lincoln, John Hay and Leonard Swett, Lincoln's law partner on the 8th Judicial Circuit and confidante, who executed certain sensitive and unpublicized missions for his friend and former partner, were riding in a carriage to the cottage at the Soldiers' Home. The subject of the conversation was the treason of general George McClellan. All of them had read the Van Lew letters but this was the first time the three of them were together. Lincoln initiated the discussion by reminding his audience that those three were the only ones in government who knew about this catastrophe and that is the way it should remain for infinity. "We must make every effort to keep the coming inevitable events, a potential massive domestic political earthquake with multiple international after shocks, down to a minor local rumble if that. McClellan must go, we know that and reasons for his dismissal, God knows, are just and plentiful but his treason must be kept secret." When the carriage reached the cottage the discussion continued in the sitting room with doors closed and orders for no disturbance.

TRIED, CONVICTED AND SENTENCED

Free flowing discussion ensued with give and take by all and Swett played the devil's advocate. No note was taken and no record of their meeting would be made. Lincoln discouraged talk of the potential horrific consequences of public exposure of such perfidy at the seat of government and its armed forces. Rather he concentrated on the matter and manner of the general's dismissal and whether or not he should be told of his being discovered as an agent of the Confederacy. Hay, his youth showing, was adamant that McClellan should be confronted, accused, dismissed in disgrace and be indicted, tried, convicted and sentenced appropriately for treason. Swett disagreed as did Lincoln who remained quiet as Swett presented his argument.

"We know that McClellan, "Little Mac," or "Little Napoleon," titles he acknowledges with undisguised admiration and unblemished pride, is afflicted with incorrigible self aggrandizement. That fact, mutually accepted even by his supporters, is essential in understanding the man, his intent, modus operandi and his ability to bring about irreparable harm to the cause, the military, the nation and this administration. He serves at the of pleasure of the Commander-in-Chief and may be relieved without cause. If that were the case the opposition in congress, the press, the military and the electorate would have a heyday. If he is dismissed with cause they would still have a heyday."

Lincoln shifted in his chair and grunted, " Perfidy portrayed as patriotism, humph; Carry on Leonard." Hay squirmed but remained silent.

Swett cleared his throat and continued. "So we're damned if we do and damned if we don't but that says nothing about our little tin soldier with clay feet and withered soul and what he could or would do. If we confront him with evidence of his traitorous conspiracy, no matter what our after-action would be, his ego would be challenged. He'd be forced to prove to himself that he was still in command and would endeavor to show he could still outsmart us. He would play the wounded crusader carrying the torch for the peace party, not a traitor but a patriot, an unsung hero. And he could do damage." He paused, looking into the eyes of his listeners.

Lincoln left his chair, deep in thought. He approached the drinks cabinet, turned and offered, "Gentlemen, some libation?"

"A bight of your Kentucky bourbon would be fine." responded Swett.

"Thank you sir, some port would be nice." replied Hay.

Lincoln poured himself half a tumbler of bourbon and as sommelier, served his co-conspirators with equal hospitality and proposed a toast. " To the Union, to us to preserve it."

"Hear Hear!" rang out from the co-conspirators.

Lincoln sat and Swett continued. "On the other hand, how best to neutralize this threat with the least amount of backlash? Remember, his secret core, his psychic image, disguised as patriotic zeal, would demand revenge. If, however, he was not relieved from command and discharged from the army but transferred to another posting deficient in critical command responsibilities and defunct of influence, he'd no doubt be quick to submit his letter of resignation. And, best of all, he'd be devoid of any need for exacting revenge upon the knaves in Washington. Because he still, in his own mind, would be surreptitious, his dissembling would be undiscovered and he would have outsmarted the Gorilla and his court of baboons in Washington."

Lincoln went for a repeat slug of bourbon and poured for the rest. "My friends, when you've got an elephant by the tail and he wants to run, you'd best let him run. It is well known among friend and foe that I've expressed and shown great displeasure regarding the general's failure to crush Lee at and after Antietam...and that I've born his burden of slowness...some say pusillanimity...others treason. So now we will put accepted, if not expected, military action into play. In the morning Stanton will be ordered to take the necessary action and he will be most pleased. And the reason for him and the world is the president's patience well has run dry." At that he emptied his tumbler, thanked his friends, shook their hands, bade them a good night and marched off to his bedroom.

Le Clarion D'Argent Muted

A little after 11:00 P.M. on 7 November, 1862, in a snowstorm, Brigadier General Catharinus P. Buckingham, under direct orders of Secretary Stanton, and in the presence of McClellan's reluctant replacement, General Ambrose Burnside, delivered the directive relieving George Brinton McClellan of his command with orders to transfer to Trenton, New Jersey and await further orders. This was most humiliating and unpleasant but no surprise to Little Napoleon, and he allowed no muscle to quiver or the slightest expression of feeling to be visible on his face..."They shall not have that triumph." as he described in his letter to Nelly. And it was not good news nor was it unexpected by Benjamin and Lee who commented, " I fear they may continue to make these changes till they find someone whom I don't understand." Judah Benjamin suffered a case of the withers for a week or so, tossed in his bed, poked at his food, growled at Jules, giving him a case of gastric distress and insomnia. But Judah was seldom seen without a half filled brandy snifter held by his pudgy fingers. He mourned the loss of that exquisite source of irreplaceable intelligence, a subterfuge the world has never known, a product of his own genius as if it were the demise of his first born. In an act of salvation he concentrated on developing his espionage operations in not only the Union but in Canada, the Caribbean and Europe... not primarily but secondarily, a safety net for his future physical, political and financial security.

Swett's hypothesis proved positive. McClellan accepted accolades, awards and honors, befitting, as he assumed, a returning conqueror of old. His military departure was greeted with mixed emotions. There were his detractors but there were still his partisans;

some in the press, a few vocal politicians and his immediate staff officer cadre who yearned for his recall. Burnside's bloody debacle at Fredericksburg, losing the battle and 12,653 troops in the process while Lee lost 5309 and Hooker's disastrous defeat at Chancellorsville, with Union losses at 16,792 compared to those of the Confederacy at 12,764, spurred those desirous of McClellan's return. But Lincoln, held firm and said no. And only he and two others in Washington knew the real reason...treason...why.

While awaiting orders that did not materialize, he worked on his report of his 15 months as commanding general of the Army of the Potomac. Aside from documents, reports, maps, dispatches and telegrams he had retained, he had his voluminous collection of letters to Nelly as source material for his report which read more like his memoirs, according to the New York Times. As a salve to his bruised ego McClellan accepted awards, honors and invitations to feted events, he even accepted a presentation sword from a citizen's committee in Boston. Stanton blocked a move by an officer group to fund a sword presentation. And, of course, as morning follows the night, a political career path never dimmed in the shadowed corridors of his mental castle...fostered by fractions of Democrats and Peace movement members who were not all kissing cousins. Eventually he was the Democrat candidate for President to run against Abraham Lincoln as indicated by his letter of acceptance of the nomination of 8 September 1864. On 8 November 1864 he was soundly defeated in the general election. Of great embarrassment and pain was the overwhelming number of votes for Lincoln by his beloved men at arms; the combatant, invalid and veteran population all favored Lincoln over McClellan by not a plurality but a significant majority. His letter of resignation from the army was accepted without hesitation or reservation. Best for all to go into exile; Europe won out over Utah or Nevada so he and his family set sail for England on 25 January 1865.

April---No Time for Fools or the Footless

On Sunday, 2 April 1865, Richmond, Virginia was aflame; columns of smoke blotted out the sun by day and the milky way and moon by night. Mobs were milling, looting and evacuating. At 10:40 A.M. that morning, General Lee wired Secretary of War Seddon advising him to evacuate Richmond. Earlier that morning A. P. Hill was killed near Petersburg by a Union bullet through his heart. In the back of the Mechanics Building at 9th & Bank Streets in Richmond a portly gentleman, choking, puffing, sweating and tremulous, with the anxiety of the occasion, approached the bonfire getting very close to the flames. He placed, rather than threw, his sheaths of documents into the inferno. His subordinates, scurrying to and fro, were just throwing their handfuls of files into the blazing pile willy-nilly. But Secretary Benjamin wanted to know without a doubt that these files were gone forever. He must be assured that history would forever be blind to their contents and that his and his other conspirators' secrets would never be revealed. He turned and went back to his preparations for his departure by train for Danville, Virginia, with President Davis and the rest of his Cabinet later that evening. Dearest Jules would not accompany the government contingent; he would be safer traveling separately with a companion chosen by Benjamin, eventually to family in New Orleans.

The heart and brains and treasure of the Confederate States of America departed their capital in the dark of night, leaving their dissipated muscle, depleted, desperate and deserted on the bleak fields surrounding Appomattox Court House. Lee surrendered formally on 12 April, 1865.

Lincoln toured Richmond and Grant had tea with Elizabeth Van Lew after he placed sentries around her mansion for her safety. Lincoln was assassinated on Good Friday, 14 April, 1865. Benjamin, as "Mephistopheles of the Rebellion, the brilliant, learned, sinister Secretary of State," was thought to be deeply involved in the plot by a number of government officials and members of the press. On 26 April, 1865, General Joseph Johnson surrendered the last Confederate force to General Sherman and John Wilkes Booth died that day, shot by army pursuers. Benjamin, separated from Davis' party in late April, got to Florida, by avoiding capture by the searching Union Army patrols by using multiple disguises and personas. Then he went by harrowing voyages with near fatal events to Bimini, Nassau, Cuba, Saint Thomas and finally to England. He arrived at Southampton, England on 30 August, 1865. and went to London to help his agent, James Mason, close business at the consulate. He was a subject of the crown because of his birth on the British Virgin Island of Saint Thomas, a crown colony, so he would be safe in England and free of extradition to the United States. He visited his wife and daughter in Paris, seeing them for the first time in five years, and declined offers of positions in the French banking circles. His reason..."Nothing is more independent, nor offers a more promising future, than admission as a barrister to the bar of London." He began law studies in London in January 1866 and was called to the bar on 6 June, of that year, after only six months as a law student, instead of the usual three years apprenticeship, arranged by influential friends in high places.

The Dimming Afterglow

In the interim, Davis and party were captured by Union Cavalry on 2 May, 1865. Jules St. Martin was captured in Montgomery, Alabama, paroled and enjoyed a loving reception into the arms of his family in their home in the safety of New Orleans. McClellan was enjoying the splendors of the continent. Nelly gave birth to their second child, a son, George Brinton McClellan Jr. on 23 November, 1865, in Dresden, Germany, his "winter quarters." Back home, he had become wealthy by 1870, enjoying a few minor appointments in local government in New York and profiting from railroad endeavors. This enabled him to construct a large rambling structure on Orange Mountain, New Jersey, Maywood, named after his first born. In 1873 he formed his own firm, Geo B. McClellan & Company to encourage and represent European investors in American railroads and returned to Europe to foster his private enterprise. In February of that year he decided to pay a visit to Judah Benjamin in London, unannounced.

A Final Bout of Benjamin

The Honourable Society of Lincoln's Inn, located in the Holborn section of London, was the center of law for English and Welch barristers where they were called to the bar. It provided "training houses" for young lawyers and in 1464 the Inn was formally organized as a place of legal education. Old Square, the closest building to the Gatehouse, built in the mid-16th century was a five stories structure with residential flats on the top floor. Barrister Judah P. Benjamin, titled Queen's Counsel in 1872, pulled apart the heavy woolen water-stained draperies to peer out his leaded fifth floor window. It was dark and dank in the fading light of dusk exacerbated by a fog rolling up Chancery Lane. At street level a lone figure wearing a beaver top hat, a long coat with upturned collar against the chill of the wind-blown damp, carrying a walking stick, strutted with a distinct military bearing. George Brinton McClellan could barely make out the tops of the Gatehouse towers secreted by a veil of mist moving as if by the hand of an unseen illusionist as he paraded up Chancery Lane and entered into the hallowed grounds of Lincoln Inn. As he climbed the well worn steps of Old Square with central depressions of the stone treads made by the boots, pumps and shoes of innumerable robed and wigged barristers of centuries past, he pulled his collar and arms closer to his body because it was colder inside Old Square than outside. And what of this more recent barrister and resident of Lincoln Inn? How coincidental and amusing in a morose sort of manner, thought McClellan, that Judah Benjamin, Mephistopheles of the rebellion, would seek solace and succor in an institution that carries the name of the man whom he had spent rivers of blood and untold treasure to defeat, demonize, unseat...abduct... yes, even assassinate. Pondering these thoughts helped alleviate his building apprehension as he climbed the steep steps to meet his old espionage controller.

On the fifth landing, a bit winded, he paused before walking the darkened hallway to the large oaken door at its end. He raised the wrought iron knocker, wrapped three times and waited. A latch sounded and the door creaked open revealing a slight plump man with a large head, wearing a heavy knitted woolen sweater, grey shapeless woolen trousers and a dark maroon knitted shawl over his stooped shoulders. He was shod in faded red carpet slippers. His mustache and beard were greyed more so than his full head of hair. His expression was timeless...that constant half smile, half smirk with tight straight lips. He allowed no evidence of shocked surprise to appear on his countenance.

Judah Benjamin opened the door widely and extended both hands that looked pale and delicate like those of a woman.

"Mon general...le clarion d'argent." The spoken language was French. "Such a great and unexpected, not to mention undeserved, honour and pleasure to see you again...and in much less precarious and threatening circumstances and environs. And I most appreciate that I am no longer in need of a disguise of an obese, obtuse, saddle-sore, French chef with a toothache."

They both laughed and shook hands.

The accommodations were cramped and sparsely furnished, a notable characteristic of the rooms of the Inns. Heavy dark drapes with water stains adorned the leaky leaded windows and were pulled to keep London's February chill outside and the meager amount of heat from the coal stove inside. A tattered carpet with threadbare footpaths lay on the wide board floor and small books, pamphlets, papers and large leather-bound volumes resided in comfort on every available flat surface including the floor. The desk was small and covered with books and papers that made it all but unidentifiable except for the Windsor chair that sat behind it and the oil lamp and spectacles resting on it. The place smelled of burning coal, lamp oil and mildewed books and had a pervasive chill. It was also not well illuminated; deep shadows predominated. No kettle or cup was apparent and no tea was offered. It was a gloomy place.

Benjamin adjusted his shawl and gestured for the general to take the wingback chair while the newly appointed Queen's Counsel took the desk chair. He faced McClellan and graced him with that same old half smile, half smirk, the expression that was so well known by all who beheld the Mephistopheles of the Rebellion.

Was it the fly in the spider's parlor or the wolf in the fox's lair? Neither was sure.

Doing away with the amenities, McClellan broke the growing tension. "There are rumors in high circles, government, mercantile and military, that there is a vast horde of gold sequestered on the continent to which you have not only access but control. This trove is the remnant of the gold sent to Europe to finance the efforts to bring England and France and any other convinced state to recognize the legitimacy of the government of the Confederate States of America and to purchase powder, weapons and vessels to prosecute the war. That depository was or those depositories were intact at the cessation of hostilities in America. Few, if any but you, knew their whereabouts and had the means to access it or them."

Benjamin leaned forward, his chair squeaked, picked up his spectacles, placed them on his nose, looked over the top of the lenses and cast a sideways glance at the general.

"Come now mon general, would I, with the wherewithal you have alleged that I have available to me, live in such humble accommodations and ply the strife-ridden life of a barrister eking out a pittance to provide sustenance for my survival and a roof over my head and fuel for my stove? Kind sir, be the man of reason

I know you to be. Look around you. Are these the lodgings and comforts of a man of wealth?"

McClellan sat fixed in gaze and posture. Not a muscle moved nor an eye shifted by a degree.

Benjamin shifted in his chair causing more intense squeaks that broke the deafening silence. He leaned on both elbows focused on the general's nasion, that point between his eyes.

McClellan. bristled. "Mr. Benjamin," spoken in a commanding tone, "let us be honest. You and I are both dissemblers...we always have been and we always will be. It is time we put aside the playacting and tomfoolery. We are now men of business. You and I have left the world of government and arms. We are both making our ways in the world of commerce. We each want something the other one has---"

"But general!" broke in the Queen's Counsel, "You are overlooking some very obvious and real points of---"

"I appeal to your courtesy sir, do not interrupt me." The general almost commanded.

"Please mon general, accept my most humble apology." intoned in his most silky voice as he tilted his head ever so slightly and affected that smile indicating he was still in control not only of himself but of his guest and the matter at hand. He sat back and the chair squeaked. "Please sir, be so kind as to enlighten me as to how we can benefit each other and make life's disappointments more acceptable and its toils more tolerable."

McClellan rose from his chair smartly, stood for a silent moment with arms akimbo, then he leaned over the desk with both arms out stretched, hands on the papers and glared at Benjamin. "I want recompense, just compensation for services rendered above and beyond all reason and sanity to you and your government. And that remuneration will also cause a silence to befall upon my lips and tongue rendering me mute in ongoing and/or future inquiries about you and your role, alleged or factual, in matters of great concern to the present and future governments of the United States"

Benjamin forced a laugh then sighed. "I am a subject of the Crown...a Queen's Counsel. I am not subject to the laws of the United States of America nor am I subject to their jurisdiction in any manner, civil or criminal. Any possibility of extradition is completely out of the question. I am safe here and anywhere in Europe. But I appreciate your most generous offer of assistance were I to need it. You have my most heartfelt gratitude. And now if you will excuse me I must, with the utmost regret and respect, request of you to take your leave."

At that, Judah P. Benjamin, former Attorney General, Secretary of War and Secretary of State of the Confederate States of America and now Queen's Counsel to the government of H.R.H. in Great Britain, crossed the room to the door, opened it and bid his guest "God Speed."

The Last Hurrah

Back in the United States, McClellan, once again entered public life. In 1877, at 50 years of age, he was elected Governor of the Garden State, New Jersey, traveling one day a week, Tuesday, from Maywood to Trenton, the state capital, conducting state business and returning home that night. It was a term of three years. He was also active in the election of President Grover Cleveland, hoping to be in his cabinet as Secretary of War. Much to his perturbation the appointment went to a political hack. Travels and multiple corporate board memberships, mining and other commercial enterprises occupied his waking hours. Between travels he wintered in New York, where McClellan receptions earned five stars on the winter social calendar, summered in Maywood except for the dog days of August, he went to Mount Desert Island, Maine and the White Mountains of New Hampshire.

Le Clarion D'Argent's Last Call...Taps

At Maywood, in early October of 1885, He suffered a severe attack of acute chest pain that responded to medical care and rest until the evening of 28 October when the chest pain returned and his condition deteriorated rapidly eventuating in his demise in the early hours of the 29th.

Maywood Mansion was darkened and alone on its Orange Mountain. It was eery, strangely quiet as the Madam retired alone to her suite, separate from "the general's." She always referred to him as, "the general" when addressing others. That was not only his wish but his order. There was no sobbing or wailing, no outburst or demonstrative grieving of any kind. The few silent tears shed were controlled by the dabbing of a laced handkerchief. The whole scene, though funereal, was one of controlled emotion, so typical of Philadelphia's social set; understated dignity of demeanor and manners. It was the norm of that set in the "City of Brotherly Love." White Anglo-Saxon Protestant predominance with no small taint of Quaker influence.

Alone with her thoughts, which were, strangely, so incongruous at this instant, of bygone days on the plains of West Point and of Ambrose. Ambrose, always Ambrose, beloved Ambrose...my first and only true love, stolen from me and then rendered unable to mourn his death in my setting. My betrothal and marriage to George was arranged as if I were a Hindu. But, at the time, I went along with it and regretted it almost daily up to the present. And now I am free of that hateful bind but Ambrose is gone and

I am alone in my own world with my children and a few true friends. Free from the outside world of George's associates and colleagues...accomplices and cronies better describes them. Their world is too much with me. Release, I need release and relief...to be alone and breathe deeply of free air and think free thoughts unencumbered by the hordes of helpers anxious to help me to help themselves.

She smiled at herself in the mirror of her dressing table. She felt little guilt for that strange but odd sense of pleasure that comes with the solace from perpetual emotional strain. It was perplexing but understandable. This feeling, this sense must be hidden from all around her. She must portray the appropriately aggrieved new widow as expected. There was much to conceal; as it was, it remains.

Nelly Marcy McClellan was no stranger to compartmentalization and dissembling in as much as the sub rosa love affair she executed undiscovered for years with A.P. Hill. Not withstanding the not so insignificant role she played in the coup de theatre concocted and executed by Judah Benjamin, with beloved Ambrose and husband George as supporting and leading actors.

She left the dressing table, went to the window and gazed out upon the color changes of autumn. "Oh Ambrose, dearest Ambrose will you ever forgive me?" And she fell to the floor sobbing.

THE SERVANTS' POSTMORTEM

After the undertaker removed the deceased, Strollins, the butler, who was called by the general, "S M," for Sergeant Major, entered the servants' lunch room next to the kitchen where they were all gathered awaiting the news and their new marching orders. They were not staff...only officers were staff...they were servants!

"Well its all over," spoken in a voice that had neither the pitch nor tone of the expected respectful sotto voce befitting a matter so grave as this. "The general is dead and gone." He gave a half smile and a gentle nod of his head.

Dixie May, the upstairs maid, the general called her "U S G," for upstairs girl, was the only one to respond. "Ah thinks he picked me cause ma name was Dixie. We all knowed he was a Johnnie reb genral in a Union suit." She chuckled. "A reb genral in a Union suit. He was a mean man, always army. We wasn't his slaves, the war fixed that and so did father Abraham but we was always under his thumb.

Ah feels sorry for Miss Nelly...Madam in front a him an his friends...keepin to herself an not sayin much, not sharin the same bed but still eatin wif each otha...sad. She don't like Jersey, too quiet, nothin stirrin. Maybe she'll smile more now."

Strollins' frown generated a short pause then she began again

"Ole father Abraham aint got no worry bout sharin a place wif him cause he aint goin up. He won't no mo need fo a USG." she snickered. "Thar aint no upstairs whar he's gone. Yeah, whar he's gone, he'll git a downstairs devil, Satan's gif forevah...and I thank ya Jesus."

EPILOGUE

The only clue, hint or reference to George Brinton McClellan's skullduggery as Le Clarion D'argent were in notes he wrote in 1866. "Few, if any, know fully the motives by which my action was influenced and the circumstances by which I was often necessarily controlled; as yet no competent person has come forward to lay before the world a full account of my career."

CPSIA information can be obtained
at www.ICGtesting.com
Printed in the USA
BVHW042202041220
594951BV00021B/800

9 781728 371436